FIRST SLEEP

Christopher Da Costa

DaCostaBooks.com

For Carmel.

CONTENTS

First Sleep

Volume One

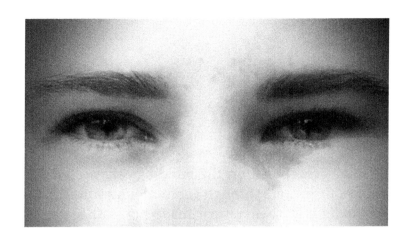

THE LAST LEFT AWAKE

"Do you know where the phrase eat, sleep and be merry for tomorrow we die comes from? The Bible. But that was yesterday. Today we're still alive and we all want to live for bigger dreams. The trouble is, if you chase your dreams and don't succeed, they begin to follow you in life..."

Wild lights danced in the dark, red, blue and white.

Are You Happy With Your Current Service?

豪华版

The adverts played on the buildings above, refracting like neon stars through Leon's cloudy windshield. His anxiety at their return made his leather gloves scrunch on the wheel. *W 4th Street.* The pencilled writing lit up in headlights as he followed the sign home, funnelled by towers touching the sky.

"Home sweet home," he said, feeling uninvited.

As he drove along the lonely street, Leon felt like the last man left awake. A distant ambience from the cars kept him daydreaming of teenage years by the LA coast, echoing waves of the ocean.

A red traffic light woke him up. He glanced in his rear view mirror for any trouble. Still empty. *03:09,* read the dashboard clock.

He pulled the mirror down to check himself. Tired eyes stared back at him with oily skin looking overexposed under street lamps. All things considered, could be worse, he thought. From mousey hair, his nails scraped down his face as he chewed over thoughts.

Have I made a mistake? Came the next one.

Upon the flicker of neon green he drove onto *Flower Street*, into dull shapes forming an elevated highway, and with it two silhouettes outside its entrance. Leon drew closer and the picture became clear: two plain-clothes detectives stood each side of the entry, with their police car parked by the curb.

Slowly he drifted his car toward them, pointlessly, they couldn't miss him.

The detective on the right made eye contact with him and held it. Tall, black, and built like a brick shithouse wearing a suit, he was not the cop Leon was hoping for. He turned and spoke to his partner, keeping Leon in his sight.

The other detective missed the memo about smart clothes in her parka and jeans. Just out of puberty with a tweenie ponytail, the girl-next-door looked bored on work experience, scuffing her boots on the ground for fun.

They were just ten metres away. Leon didn't have time for this.

The male detective stepped into the road and held out his hand in a stop signal, walking up beside the car he put his head through the open passenger window. The vapour of the detective's breath blew inches from Leon's face. He smelt yesterday's dinner and glanced up at a sinking scowl and Action Man features - a chiselled jaw, heavy brow and a round nose bent flat. Wired eyes locked onto Leon's, but he waited for the detective to speak.

"Excuse me sir," barked the Detective, "we're conducting traffic stops, where've you been tonight?"

He flashed his badge and held his stare, trying to measure him, Leon thought, as he kept eye contact.

"I've been driving from Lost Hills to here," Leon lied.

The detective's frown fell like a landslide, "I suppose you haven't heard about the commotion around here tonight then?" he interrogated.

"Not at all," Leon told the truth.

"Denzel," shouted the female Detective, stood in front of the police car, with a transmitter covering her mouth.

Denzel leant back and reluctantly released his grip on the car door.

"You wait here," he instructed Leon and broke contact. "What Max?" Denzel yelled as he marched towards her.

She pulled Denzel in close and whispered beside his ear, glancing at Leon and pointing toward the licence plate. Leon tightened his grip on the wheel.

Denzel snapped his head back toward Leon and swung the transmitter to his mouth, "White Male. Twenties. Green eyes. Slim build," Leon lip read, "black Chevrolet Camaro, lice-"

First gear, accelerator – clutch. He raced towards the highway. Second gear. The detectives lunged toward the passenger-side with their hands as he passed them.

Third gear. Why do they always think they can stop a car by grabbing it? He thought.

Fourth gear. In his rear mirror he saw the cops run back to their vehicle. Fifth gear. Sixth gear. The lines on the highway and its tall metal barriers passed as one shape, and the centre focus pulled his stray thoughts inward.

The red and blue cop car became mere specks of light in his background, as he took a sharp right turn at the road's end, drifting across the street. Only two vehicles were on the road, thank fuck, he thought.

He weaved in and out of lanes, between the cars and accelerating beyond them, swivelling down narrow side streets. The towers were replaced with houses empty of light, leaving Leon in darkness but for energy saving street lamps.

With his rear view mirror empty he relaxed his grip on the wheel, following the arching road downhill, slowing to allow a speeding car cross the intersection. A hundred metres ahead the path dwindled into black. He switched off the car lights, planning to ride quietly into the night and lose the police here.

From the glovebox he reached for a cigarette, though the filter had barely touched his lips, when a noise of sirens broke in the distance. He checked all his mirrors. No sign. The sky was clear. Still the noise became a crescendo. Until the sound felt like it was exploding between his ears and beacons of red and blue lights grew from the darkness. A police car hurtled out of nothing toward him. In his back window Leon saw a side street, three hundred metres away on the right. With the pedal to the metal he set the car in reverse. Still the police car closed on him rapidly. *65 mph* read the dial, "almost," he whispered.

The car kissed Leon's bonnet, its lights nigh blinding. Past them, he saw the police officer. Grey and scared, the old man imitated a corpse, with his jaw hanging free and his body raised rigid against the seat. Pale pupils recoiled in terror, like his own death shone in the headlights.

The police car rammed him good but Leon held the car straight. This was not his first rodeo.

He checked over his shoulder. It was time. He let the police car hit him again and with its arrival turned the steering wheel all the way left. The car spun and the colours of the world ran onto each other like cheap dye. With a Rockford turn complete Leon stabilised the car into the side road. He watched the police car skate past the exit in his wing-mirror, and listened to its steel crash against something harder, feeling like his favourite movie stars.

Leon drove four blocks, between intertwining roads and beneath the cover of buildings into a shopping mall parking lot. He climbed up to the second floor and parked the Chevrolet in a corner. Out of the trunk, he grabbed a Dallas Cowboys cap and brown leather jacket and threw them on, slipping out amongst the angry sirens. Welcome home, he thought.

DO YOU OFTEN THINK ABOUT DEATH?

29th APRIL 2018

Interview 7 - 8:45AM

She sat like she was praying.

Her head was bowed, her hands clasped and her knees pointed inward. In the centre of the room, she balanced on the edge of her seat. Up at the camera, she showed the glimpse of a young face, one of olive skin craving sunlight.

The glance was brief.

She returned to staring at white ballet flats. The tattered things matched her strap vest, which like her dark skinny jeans clung to a slim figure. Yet the spotlight etched an unfinished picture. Still as a painting, she hid from the light above, beneath the bangs of long brown hair. Alone, on the white canvas of the wall.

"Good afternoon," called the Doctor behind the camera.

"Hi," she mumbled politely.

"Just for the recording, please state your name and date of birth."

"Ellie Antonova, November 20th 1996."

Ellie lifted her head to look into the lens with light blue eyes and for a moment her gaze was fixed. Into focus came a button nose, elfin ears and finely arched eyebrows. Parts felicitous in softness, and of no importance to her confidence. In an undecided expression, she turned from being watched.

"So Miss Antonova," the Doctor dropped his voice into professional mode, "my name is Dr Robert Radford, and we'll begin with the standard questions... When did you begin to feel unwell?"

From behind a desk half the room away, the Dr's face was pensive. Two caterpillar brows moved closer over a red roman nose.

Left then right she tapped her foot in another world, while the standard blueprint for a middle aged psychiatrist waited.

Back and forth his wedding ring grazed over a Freudian beard while he watched the clock. The two strangers looked everywhere around the office but at each other, until his beady spectacles really paid attention to her childlike behaviour.

She shrugged her shoulders to buy more time, pressed her lips together and exhaled, "I don't know."

"Then tell me, Ellie, how are you feeling now?"

"Like I need a Frappuccino," she joked, but neither of them laughed, "I guess it's always the same thought that I'm wasting my life," her words escaped.

Porcelain teeth scraped along her bottom lip.

"But I don't even have anything to be sad about," she said.

"It says in my notes that you currently work as an Administrator for the Alliance Corporation, how is that?"

"Pretty standard."

Dr Radford leant over the desk to get a little closer.

"One of the reasons I ask Ellie is that nothing stands out in your notes. I've got nothing here about previous psychiatric visits. Your entire hospital notes consist of appendicitis at age fifteen. Your CV is, as you say pretty standard. Good school grades and then this steady job for the last three years. So, Ellie, my real question is, what has changed in your daily life?"

"Okay I guess we're really jumping into it," she laughed nervously.

She brushed the thick hair from her face, sat upright, and consciously exhaled again, "Like I said I don't really know why I'm sad. It's just always the same day. I can wake up feeling great and dance around the house to Beyoncé, but every night I'll go to sleep feeling lost."

"You mentioned feeling like you were wasting your life," Dr Radford guided her, "what would your dream life look like?"

"It's embarrassing really..."

She chucked her hands in the air jovially, with watering eyes exposing the fake smile.

"It is for everyone to say it out loud, don't worry," he said.

"I actually thought I'd be a writer at one point, but everything came out wet and pretentious. And apparently you can't sell poetry nowadays – who knew? But what am I going to do instead, take up swimming again?" she ridiculed.

The guise finally broke.

"The truth is," she said to herself, "I don't want any more boyfriends trying to fix me so that I can just let them down. And my parents... I spent my whole teenage years trying to iron out all my flaws, thinking one day I'll get the chance to show the real me. Then I got old and realised I had nothing to offer. My parents, they emigrated from Ukraine and had to struggle. But sometimes I envy them. Because at least they had an excuse, I had every opportunity. And in the end, I listened to what my parents told me: I was just a teenager who couldn't handle her emotions properly. And I bought into their view that what I was living, what I was feeling, was actually no big deal. And soon the daydreams became 'what's for lunch?' Rather than 'what am I *doing* with my life?' So I got this job and a routine. But the problem is, the more I pretend it's fine, the more I don't know who I am."

Ellie choked on the words with eyes shut and opened them crying, "It doesn't go away," she said trying to wipe the tear.

"Do you often think about death?"

"Sometimes every day," said Ellie.

"And do you think about suicide?"

"I don't even believe I really want to die, otherwise I'd be dead. I just want to jump in front of a train or fall three thousand feet to feel something different."

Interview 10 – 11:05AM

He slouched back on the chair like he owned the place.

But he didn't make much of an impression. His baggy clothes commanded more attention, with wiry limbs stretching out of camo cargo pants and a creased t-shirt, leaving room for everyone else to misjudge him.

"Do you like my t-shirt? I wore it for you."

His hoarse voice bounced off the walls and returned to a leering smile.

Dr Radford saw the t-shirt he was pointing at, in particular the words *Man is dead*, but he chose to ignore him.

His dusty pupils winced at the rejection. But the Dr observed the faint shadows along his brow, unmoved, with hairs too thin to count.

Keen to keep the act moving along, Donnie moved his attention to the camera, blowing a fake kiss. The tiny mouth barely reached the edges of his flat nose, with thin lips fading into anaemic skin. And for all his theatrics, he could not hide his real thoughts. For when the smile dropped the camera caught the emptiness of his natural expression - just for a second.

"Good morning," spoke Dr Radford, "for the purpose of the recording, please state your name and date of birth."

"Donnie Evans. Twenty eight." he shot back.

"So Mr Eva-"

"Donnie," he interrupted.

"Yes - Donnie," continued the Dr unfazed, "we shall begin with a few simple questions. So tell me, when did you begin to feel unwell?"

"Unwell?" Donnie laughed sensationally, kicking his legs in the air. When he'd had enough fun he lurched forward in his seat. With his chin resting in his hand he mimicked Dr Radford's pose, judging him back. Still the only rise he got out of the Dr was a disinterested eyebrow.

Donnie stroked his slicked back hair. Jet black with grease. With squinted eyes he nodded sarcastically, saying, "Perhaps I just hear a different drummer." And the conceited smile returned.

"Are you depressed Donnie?" asked the Dr.

"No."

"Then why are you here?"

"Do you believe in God?" Donnie answered.

"I haven't quite made my mind up," he lied to let Donnie lead the conversation.

Donnie clapped his hands and rubbed them together like a cartoon villain.

"Me neither," said Donnie gleeful, "but do you know what the difference between me and you is? If the

Devil shot out of smoke and offered you fifty years of extra life for your soul, you'd take it before you'd even asked if he and God were pen pals."

Greeted with silence Donnie grasped the invitation to continue, "I'm not so desperate to hang onto this life as the rest of you. You know I saw a documentary the other day which said we're close to curing ageing. But let me tell you, one day you're going to step out of your box, fall down some fucking stairs, contract some coronavirus or get stabbed by a fucking junkie like me. How far do you have to go to avoid that fact? You see one person like me who wants to avoid the hassle and you can't compute. I mean I don't even mind being on suicide watch, I like the company. But if I jumped in front of a train all you would hear is 'watch the gap.' What I do care about is the self-righteousness of people like you telling me things are okay so you feel alright. I mean what the fuck do you live for really? Baseball?"

"First, I'd rather you tell me why you don't want to live?" said Dr Radford.

"Because I can't live freely."

"Get a job," Donnie cried, "repay your society." He caught up with his last sentence before the Dr could comment, laughing with himself hysterically, teary eyed.

"I can just hear my father now shouting those punchlines," Donnie's joke continued, but as his breaths slowed his words became bitter, "it is a fact that one in ten thousand of us can make a technological breakthrough capable of supporting all the rest. Yet we persist with this Malthusian-Darwinian theory that we must justify our right to exist. First you won't let me live, and now you want me to beg you to die? Fuck you."

"What is freedom to you, Donnie?"

"How does a goldfish in a bowl know what the sea is?" he said.

"Maybe a goldfish wouldn't ask that question Donnie."

"Maybe I'm not who you want me to be."

"You seem a little confused on the matter Donnie," patted the Dr's words.

Donnie's eyes grew like golf balls.

"Are you hearing the words I'm saying?"

Around an empty office, Donnie looked for support, but the audience laughter happened only in his head.

"And will you stop saying my fucking name," begged Donnie.

"What would make you happy?"

"Do you like my t-shirt? I wore it for you."

"What would make you happy?"

"I want to run out naked into the street and scream, I'm a black gay fat chick and no one bats an eyelid."

"Then you should move to South Beach."

"That's funny," laughed Donnie, but with the chuckle on mute, "I'm tired of the jokes though," he said.

"What jokes?"

Donnie let the question hang, staring at the ground he clicked his tongue and the muscles of his face finally relaxed.

"The ones that think I'm a joke. The wisecracks that assume I'm just a dumb spoilt shit who doesn't know what it's really like. I know you've heard this Gen Z hippie speech before. And I'm tired of hearing myself aloud too. But let me tell you, not rolling the dice on your Monopoly board isn't the same as losing. I'm bored of reading Plato and seeing nothing but four walls. All while the eye on the wall stares down at me, ticking away the seconds of my life, as I live another day in futility, playing doctor with you."

Interview 16 - 3:01PM

"Mrs Fields," called a voice, but she remained unmoved.

In a bubble of her own thoughts, the outside world stayed out of focus. And the words drowned out like they travelled through water.

She sat like she was waiting for someone. Arms crossed and watching the shut door.

"Mrs Fields," Dr Radford called.

She blinked with eyes set deep, draped by the sagging skin of her brow. A lavender vein flowed through the dark circles below, dwindling in pallid skin. Cracks rose from the ashen desert, and a scab lay upon her lavender lips - the sole colour in a face drained of everything else.

The Dr had stopped calling her name, getting drawn into staring with her.

Clumps of grey hair sprouted from her head, but it

was her bald eyebrows which drifted his imagination along.

He watched her face cling loosely to her skeletal bones, like a falling mask, and the shadows spread deeply between the gaps left behind.

"Mrs Bridget Fields, I am your Doctor," he shouted to wake them both up.

At once her whole body leapt backwards. "Oh, you frightened me," she laughed wildly, with her sunken eyes growing far and wide.

"Good afternoon," he said relieved.

"Yes good afternoon to you," she matched his politeness.

"How are you today Mrs Fields?"

"Very well thank you," she nodded with her eyes to the door.

"Aren't you warm in that coat?"

"Oh this," she said, pointing to a brown, thick plaid jacket that she wore with a scarf, "it's only light. This is just a summer coat."

"As long as you are comfortable. So tell me, when was it you started feeling unwell?"

"Oh, just the other day now. I have these terrible pains in my back. Terrible," she yelled, "I don't suppose you have a magic wand for me, Doctor?"

Dr Radford took in her Wicked Witch smile and saw the sweet old lady behind it.

"Mrs Fields, you've been referred to me by your carers, to be part of a study about suicide ideation. Have you ever thought, or threatened to kill yourself?"

"No, no, no," she recanted, shaking the thought of it out of her head.

"Mrs Fields, could you tell me, what is the date today?"

"Um," she smiled uneasily, showing bright square dentures and a crumble of chicken, "do you know I've forgotten now David, what date is it?"

"Guess."

"August," she said distressed.

"Mrs Fields today's date is the twenty-ninth of April."

"No. I don't think so. Are you sure?" she rallied, with her eyes searching the room for help.

The Dr felt guilty at her despair, but he had to do his job.

"Why did you call me David?"

"David? David is my husband. Have you met him? I would do anything for David. Where is he?"

"Mrs Fields I am going to say three words," he recited from his script, "and I'd like you to repeat them back for me when I stop, okay? Flower. Cake. Cat."

"Flower, cake... pussycat, pussycat, where've you been? I've been up to Lon-don to vi-sit the queen, pussycat, pussycat, where did you go?" she sung like nobody was listening.

"Meow."

WHY ARE YOU BACK?

Glass beer jugs clinked together, and the rowdy men who drank from them filled the background with roars of laughter. Leon sat with his back to the noise at the bar, looking down at the top's worn surface - thinking about nothing in particular.

"Would you like a drink?" asked the bartender.

Over Leon scowled a fat, Scottish-sounding bald man, with goblin features and ragged black beard. His lip curled waiting for a response.

"No thank you, I'm waiting for someone."

The bartender grunted and went to serve the rowdy customers in the corner. "Captain Blackbeard," they unimaginatively shouted in chorus.

The joint was old-fashioned. Varnished wood fitted the entire interior, with everything between them carrying an indistinct smell of dampness. A purpose-less number of liquor bottles hung from the bar, with clouded timeworn whiskeys left untouched.

Leon caught his reflection in the mirror behind the

bottles.

The dim spotlights drew faint shades over his cheek-boned face and washed out scars, along the line thread from the edge of his thin lips, and the other scratched under his right eyebrow. They were barely noticeable, still he paid attention to them. Some of them were from good times.

Twenty six years old and a five o'clock shadow of a man. The kind of guy that when he turned eighteen, his parents moved out. At least that's the kind of jokes Vincent would make. The truth is, he was just detached from the melodrama that carried life around him. The pretty couple who were passive aggressively breaking up in the corner. The beer bellied rabble making love to their peanuts over the fruit machine. And the queue of people who were elbowing him for space at the bar. Yet he was jealous all the same.

Sometimes he blamed his parents. Deliberately, he ran his fingers through the thick hair his mother gave him, down onto the bridge of his nose - checking it felt straight. He'd broken his nose so many times he developed the habit. In the mirror, he noticed a flake of dried blood clinging onto his pointed left ear. He just hoped he hadn't left any in the car for the police.

Above the bar played an old television:

A cartoon kid with spikey hair held onto the back of a cowboy, and together they rode a horse away from the chasing waves. With a jolt of the cowboy's brick-shaped chin, he quipped, *"Hold on tight Jimmy."*

"But how will we escape the milk?" squeaked the kid.

"I've got it Jimmy," said the Cowboy, *"we'll use Sheriff John's Honeycomb Crisp to soak it all up,"* And with a crescent smile and steely eyes he pulled a box of cereal from his waist-coat.

Jesus Christ these adverts, thought Leon. Childhood viewings of For a Few Dollars More replayed Clint Eastwood lines in his head, before he remembered his impending meeting with Vincent. He checked the time on the TV, but instead, the bulletin caught his attention:

Doomsday Approaches: But Why This Time?

"– This time it's David Meade's turn to throw a dart at the clock with May 2018. But hey, after we made it through 2012 I'm surprised anyone even notices these predictions anymore," spoke an uppity middle-aged woman. Her craggy face and purple blazer reminded Leon of his old science teacher.

> *"But then again it's not too surprising, when we put the recent attention to claims the world is going to end into context. So many of us seem to sense the end of something; we just can't place it. Maybe for old people it's moral values? For the young good job prospects? And for people like me in the middle, it's a sensible argument. But in any case, it all stems from our paranoia."*

Leon returned to staring at the bar's worn top.

"Well I'm sorry to bring an end to this discussion," announced the News Anchor, *"But Diana has the latest*

weather where you are. No locusts or Four Horsemen I hope Diana?"

The heavy door of the bar slammed shut, and over his shoulder appeared Vincent. He strutted into the room like it was his stage, bowling his walk in slow motion, and nodding hello with a creepy smile. He hasn't changed, thought Leon, including his thrift shop fashion. This cat walk included an old green hoody two sizes too big, flared jeans and his beloved timberland boots.

"Have you been waiting long?" asked Vincent, in his version of a New York accent.

"About twenty minutes."

To Leon, Vincent always sounded like he was talking with his mouth full. He had known him since his punk-rock phase age eleven, through the teenage Rastafarian years, to whatever the fuck this was. He wondered at the ridiculous goatee and the blow dried black hair in a top knot, and said, "But I was expecting more of a Bob Marley looking guy."

The new look did distract from Vincent's overgrown facial features, which looked like a classic fancy dress disguise missing the glasses.

"Oh you like the new vibe?" cackled Vincent, "Let's find a quiet corner."

"Yeah, you seem ready to order an avocado milkshake and talk about being vegan."

They sat in a secluded cubicle far from the rowdy men, who were joined by the bartender, in drinking, and in the shouting of an unintelligible song.

"So how have you been man?" cried Vincent.

"Good. You?"

"Ah, I don't know, business is okay, but this city man. It's tiring you know."

Vincent was relieved to say it aloud.

"Recruitment is good," he continued, "got a couple youngsters coming up. But it's all small fry lately man, and you know me, I'm still trying to catch the big one."

Vincent rocked his head back and forward, waiting for Leon to say something. He did not.

"I see the scar on your lip is gone," blurted Vincent, "so you can finally stop making me feel guilty about that now."

"I don't know about that, the memory of you running away hasn't faded."

"The kid was a beast, man," Vincent replied, failing to gesticulate a monster.

"The fourteen year old?"

"So, older than us. Plus the kid had a knuckle duster - more fool you for being a good friend really."

As Vincent flicked a finger gun and winked with what could have been a stroke, Leon wondered how they were ever friends.

"I can agree with that," he said.

"But speaking of business, since you brought up the subject," Vincent hijacked the conversation, "I wondered if you might help me out. These - "

"No."

"You haven't even let me finish," Vincent whined, "an important friend of mine will be coming into town

for a delivery and in need of protection. Weapons pro-
vided, big money upfront."

"I'm not interested," Leon deadpanned him.

Insulted, Vincent threw his hand in the air like a
pissed toddler, and up with them went his voice,
"Come on man hear me out, it's been like two years
since I've seen you - I hear you're back, I make a point
to see you, I offer you good money no strings attached.
What's the deal? You still think you're too good for
this?"

Leon welcomed the sulk with a half-smile of amuse-
ment and an endless feeling of déjà vu. "Vincent," he
said calmly, "I've been back in this city five minutes,
and already you're trying to get me in jail. And not just
with any job, but with some drug deal no doubt. You
know I got chased into the city? It could have been for
just an unpaid speeding ticket or it could have been for
you know what. For years I've told you you're in too
deep, why would I be interested now?"

Vincent thought about throwing another tantrum
but deflated into a giddy state.

"Hey, alright man," he said with a mouth full of
jagged teeth, "my bad. There's always somebody else,
it's fine. I ain't even mad. Just would have been nice
to have you around some more. But I don't get it man,
why are you back?"

PHOSPHENES

5th MAY

With closed eyes Leon listened to the faint sound of footsteps from the outside corridor, tapping in rhythm. In their familiar sound he tried to muse his thoughts to a nicer place.

None of comfort came to mind.

He sat next to the reason for his return. Mrs Fields, or as he liked to call her, his good old Nan. They rubbed shoulders below the sign *WAITING AREA*, along a row of plastic seats. Surrounded by equally inanimate strangers, in what could have been The Walking Dead does musical chairs. He peered across at jittering hands, purple skin and bandages - back to her, smiling to say everything was okay.

She remained unmoved. Hunched forwards, and staring into empty space.

Leon knew he could not help her anymore, but the habit comforted him.

Plastered against the facing wall was a poster:

Educate, Provide and Recognize. Dementia edu-

cation can help people living with these con-
ditions, their families and caregivers. It's our
goal to present resources and programs that can
make a difference in your life, and other people's
lives.

Leon looked back at her still gawking at air. Playing out a pretty picture, he hoped, in the thoughts he could not know.

His eyes followed her lavender vein down to her drooping jowls, thinking, this is all to be expected. But how had he let his Nan go through Dementia by herself? Leon's mind continued, all the while thinking he was the lonely one.

He stared again at the lines on her face, formed by countless expressions of laughter and grief. So worn by the years, that with a new smile they neither rise nor fell anymore, but remain held in time.

"Mrs Fields," a doctor called from the adjacent doorway.

"That's us, let's go," spoke Leon, placing his hand on her shoulder.

"Oh Leon, you frightened me. I was half asleep," his grandma laughed wildly, with her face jumping to life.

"Where are we going?"

"The Doctor is waiting for you, just in here."

Leon led the way and she followed his footsteps, as Dr Radford headed the conga line through a narrow hallway. Spotlights passed overhead. The Dr's shoes squeaked. He was fairly short, around 5'8" Leon con-

sidered. Probably mid-fifties. His shirt too big and his
belt too small for his waist. Leon measured him up
like he did most people - without even realising. A
bald-spot on the back of the Dr's head drew his focus,
as he followed him into the office.

 The Dr swivelled onto his leather seat, behind a desk
keeping patients at a distance.

 "Mrs Bridget Fields, nice to see you again," said Dr
Radford with a smile, made genuine through the con-
viction of his beady eyes.

 "Yes good afternoon to you Doctor," his Nan recited
in her best posh voice.

 "Please, take a seat," he returned the pleasantries,
motioning her towards the armchair.

 Back into the cushions she fell, crossing her arms
upon landing.

 "I'm Dr Robert Radford. I conducted Mrs Field's interview last week, and I'll continue to be your first point
of call. I'm your new personal consultant, punch bag,
and all around stress reliever. I'll take care of you."

 His voice was a baritone with a Chicago twang, left
unanswered. Leon was like a mute bodyguard by the
door and his grandma was too busy catching flies.

 The Dr brushed off the rejection, repeating his question from last week, "Aren't you warm in that coat,
Mrs Fields?"

 "Oh this," she said, pointing to a thick plaid jacket
that she wore with a scarf, "it's only light. This is just a
summer coat."

 "Mrs Fields," Dr Radford said pensive, "tell me then,

how are you feeling today?"

"Oh, I have these terrible pains in my back. Terrible," she yelled, "I don't suppose you have a magic wand for me, Doctor?"

His reply was ready, "I suppose if I reach deep into my back pocket I might have something to help with the pain," he acted out a grin, "however, it states in my notes that you have been feeling a little depressed, is this true Mrs Fields?"

"No," her scowl batted the question away, "no, that's not me."

"It says here," continued Dr Radford, "that the Setting Sun Care Home, acting on your behalf, has referred you to me for help."

"Oh does it? Well, if it says it there maybe," she laughed shakily, "they are lovely people at that home you know. They are, the nicest people."

"Yes, Mrs Fields, could you tell me, what is the date today?"

"Um," she laughed with a forced ha ha, "do you know I've forgotten now, Leon what date is it?"

"The 5th of May," Leon saved her.

"Ah yes, the 5th of May 2014," she said defiantly. So proud that she continued into rhyming scat singing, "And I've been to Lon-don to vi-sit the queen, do-do ha ha."

Dr Radford and Leon shared a silent glance across the room, each waiting to see how the other reacted. With Leon's indifference, the Dr understood the singing wasn't too different at all from her normal behaviour.

"That's a beautiful voice," said Dr Radford with extra cheer, until his demeanour hardened talking to Leon, "I would like to set another appointment for her. Firstly, to see how her condition progresses. And, I don't know if anybody has mentioned this to you Leon, but she'll be getting some therapy as part of a study we're running."

"What kind of study?"

"It's a research study involving a series of interviews with patients who have become depressed or disillusioned with their daily lives. Put simply, we're trying to gain more insight into the common reasons people become unhappy, across multiple age groups," answered Dr Radford, avoiding the word 'suicidal.'

"That doesn't sound simple at all."

"Quite right boy," said Dr Radford impressed. And after a tic of his bushy brow, he became jovial again, "In the meantime, I'm just a call or email away."

"Okay Doc."

"Okay Mrs Fields," said Dr Radford, "so, I'll see you soon."

"God bless you too Doctor," she declared. Even making the effort to shuffle over and shake his hand.

"And peace be with you," he replied without thinking. Embarrassed, he hurriedly said to Leon, "Sorry, old Catholic habits coming back there."

Leon was just glad to see his Nan confuse somebody else. "Don't worry," he said, "I find it's like talking to an Alexa."

Leon nodded to say thanks as they left – but closing the door slowly, his grandma didn't miss the chance for one last wide smile through the gap. Dr Radford waited for her to say, "Here's Johnny," but thankfully she belted out, "I'll see you soon," instead.

The door shut and Dr Radford could release the laughter.

"Reminds me of my mother," he muttered.

He signed off her form: *R. Radford*, shuffled his papers, and stretched out his arms yawning - contemplating the photo on his desk. Back at Dr Radford smiled his younger self. He held his arm around his wife with her hand resting in his. She mimicked his stock-photo grin with perfect teeth and sapphire eyes. A child sat on his knee, with snow skin and white blonde hair - cut short with a terribly straight fringe. A runny nose and chubby cheeks ran wide with laughter and two blue gem stones let everyone know she was her mother's daughter. The girl hugged Dr Radford's leg, and he leant back in his chair, letting the memory play out a little longer.

"Home time," he stuttered through the yawn still going.

18:04, read the clock.

Dr Radford leapt to his feet and walked out, switching off the lights as he left. Spotlights passed overhead - his shoes squeaked on the floor. Twice he sniffed at the air to be sure it was just bleach.

"Are they trying to make us all patients?" he mumbled.

His heavy hands swung open a door to a vast globular space - the centre of the adjoining corridors, and a whole world of phenolic resin plastic. He stood outside the desk of Reception, shouting, "Maggie I'm going home," into an empty booth.

"Goodbye, fingers crossed for the game tonight," fired back a high-pitched nasal howl from round the corner.

"Oh don't worry, we've got this," Dr Radford said to himself.

He continued his walk out of the exit doors and collided with fervent heat, steering his face through layers of heavy air, catching his breath through taste-tests of humidity.

The sun's rays reflected off the parked cars and in three steps Dr Radford's glasses were a prism for white light. Through muscle memory he made it further along the sidewalk, fumbling the order of an Uber, falling into the sanctuary of air conditioning two minutes later.

"Maple Street, Bellflower – right boss?" said the driver's sad eyes from the rear mirror.

'Right," he said.

4.84 rated Jesse ruined his chances for a 5-star review, when he not only left the window open but turned up the car radio.

"*By Migos and Cardi B*," announced the DJ.

Of course, Dr Radford didn't do anything but listen with the wind in his hair.

"We bring you breaking news that Khloé Kardashian is sticking by baby daddy Tristan Thompson. This is despite the widespread rumours of his cheating, and following the birth of their somewhat uniquely named baby, True."

How original, he thought.

His attention returned to the outside world. With his head rest against the glass, he switched off the noise, watching the countless cars move behind each other. Ants in a line. One at a time, in a two second sequence. Every morning and evening they passed. The return of his screen saver. His eyes closed.

"Wakey wakey sir, you're home," said Jesse. Who got a 5-star review after all.

Dr Radford stepped out, noticing the Range Rover parked across the driveway. It was a three bedroom detached house with a pool, and tonight a setting sun above. With brogue shoes waking up the sleepy suburb he strolled to the front door with his hands by his side, brushing the flowers beside the path, whistling to Cardi B.

He entered with the command, "Keep the TV off, I don't want to know the score."

High white walls and high school pictures of him and his wife greeted him home. Lit up by a sphere chandelier, reflecting off stone marble floor.

He clunked his way into the living room, to see the woman from the picture standing before him. And to him, his wife Jean was as radiant now as ever.

"It's off for God's sake," she said with a Chicago twang.

"Just checking, and how has your day been?"

"Long and tiring," she answered, and they kissed with a peck.

"Oh good, one of your better days then," he joked.

With the TV remote appearing in his grasp, his butt dropped on a cream sofa.

"Ha. Ha. That'd be funny if it wasn't true."

"I see you've started without me," he said, pointing to a glass of wine on the window sill.

"You mean you missed the start."

She wedged herself in beside him on the sofa, one hip at a time, touching knees.

"We need a bigger sofa," he said, through breaths pretending to choke.

"Or you need to lose some weight," Jean fired with a high eyebrow.

"There was plenty of room before you sat down that's all I'm saying."

Her fist jabbed his leg.

"What time do you call this anyway?"

"I know," he answered, holding her hand, and with great effort said, "It was a long, long day."

Jean stole the TV remote to press un-mute:

"High May temperatures of 86 degrees as the Senator addressed - "

"But actually I haven't even told you about my day yet," Jean's voice cut off the reporter, "well, remember how I told you about how Sophie and Elliott have fallen out over Richard's report and I'm in the middle of all of it, well - "

Dr Radford's thoughts floated away, with his attention straddling the words, "Sophie started to cry," and the flashing colours of the television. His focus blurred until his mind absorbed the phosphenes that swam before him.

"Do you think we watch too much TV?" spoke Dr Radford.

"What? Not really, we're barely here. Why?" she replied confused.

"Nothing really. Just something a patient told me the other day. I mean, these kids are treating life like it's an essay question. And they get angry at me when I try to tell them there aren't correct answers behind my clipboard."

"Okay I guess we're talking about your work," said Jean rolling her eyes.

"Well you know what I think," she said, "the next generation always rebel. We did and I'm pretty sure we thought we had it the worst as well. Don't take it personally Robert."

"I don't take it personally," he said flustered, "it's just

when we were young rebelling was the fun part. These kids, they're just so lonely."

"Three quarters of Facebook users are as active or more since privacy scandal-"

"Well there's your answer," said Jean.

Dr Radford wilted back on the sofa, "I guess," he said with a pretend smile.

"But seriously. You're a great psychiatrist and I won't let you wallow like this."

"It's just sometimes it feels like I need to give them the benefit of growing old first to know better. Except they may not make it. Unless I get through to them. But they don't believe anything I say, and even if I had proof they'd just get all existential on me. They get tired of asking the big questions and feeling like they're the only ones thinking about them, whilst we go about our mundane daily routine, not realising, we're in the same position as them, just making the most of things."

"Okay you're a great psychiatrist in need of some counselling," she said between gulps of wine, "but why don't you just say all that to them?"

"I guess I could, except, I'm not sure agreeing the world is fucked up is the best idea for changing their minds about it."

"Well, I disagree entirely."

Dr Radford enjoyed these chats. As even when he didn't make much sense, she could always find something to say which levelled him to a calmer mood.

"Well maybe we should swap jobs for a day," he said.

"You couldn't handle being a real doctor," she said for the 1000th time in thirty two years. And still enjoying it.

You would think after so many years he would've had a good comeback, but the TV saved him instead:

> *"The Boston Red Sox emphatically beat Rangers tonight 5-1, hitting four homers off 44 year old right-hander Bartolo Colon-"*

"Well," he announced, falling further back in his seat, "I guess I don't need to watch the game after all."

"You've done it again haven't you," revelled Jean, giving him side-eye across the sofa.

"Me?" his voice hit the ceiling.

Dusk gave way to darkness. And still they squabbled through the night in front of the TV lights. In a street lined with homes, the windows took turns to blinker. Yet when Dr Radford's head finally hit the pillow, the brightest lights were dancing behind his eyes, in the phosphenes, returned to haunt him, with dreams of failure and fear.

Nothing here ever truly rests.

A SAD PORTRAIT

6th MAY

Fuck, thought Leon.

He slept fully clothed in an armchair beside the bed. Same jeans and denim jacket on as yesterday, ruining a cream carpet with muddy boots.

But who's going to see it anyway? He reasoned to himself, drunk last night.

Passing planes and tweeting birds crept in on the room's silence, making muffled sounds outside the window. But he wasn't moving. He'd already set a new alarm for ten more minutes.

Leon left his apartment the way he had bought it five years ago. As a showcase room with cream everything: the armchair, carpet, lampshade and sofa included. Because he didn't really care. The tower block stood shoulders with the city and the place was silent at night. That was good enough and 'good enough' was how he lived lately.

He beat the annoying alarm clock to the punch - *11:00* read his iPhone.

Leon had a shower, brushed his teeth to empty

thoughts and peered past the steam on the mirror – still tired. He left the wannabe 70s look behind, chucked on a white tee and took the elevator down to the basement parking lot.

Gone was his favourite fifth generation Chevrolet Camaro, crushed in Walter Dern's scrapyard. Replaced by the most popular car in California, and the most boring vehicle ever made on four wheels. A Honda Civic. He didn't even have the new model, just a white Sedan from 2009. But most importantly, it was inconspicuous.

He drove out of the dark beneath a baby blue sky. Windows down and Ray-Bans on. Ready, he thought, for the thousand noises crashing against each other. The over lapping concrete, people and metal which fought for space. Elegant in motion, with aggressive intent. Between the reflective buildings, which beneath the sun and with a hangover, felt like the inside of a magnifying glass.

He left the swarm of traffic to take the long way round on an open highway, missing the countryside. Radio off, turning down all the noise.

But even that didn't calm him.

Cars passed as shapes in a kaleidoscope of strange thoughts. And before he was ready, he arrived. Through the car window Leon faced the care home he paid for. It was a converted house, tucked in-between homes, but from the outside had no obvious sign of being any different.

"Round two," he said to himself.

Leon made his entrance up the gravel path – opening the door just by leaning on it - but the hallway Reception was empty.

Dry chatter echoed out of a closed door at the end of the hall.

On his way towards the noise, he scribbled *John Smith* across a wall-hanging register. And quietly, edged the door open, inch by inch – but the hinges had other ideas.

The creaking nose went down like a wet fart in the room.

Mouths gaped. Limbs tremored. And an IV drip swung in the silence, as quivering pupils met Leon through the door ajar. But it was only a group of old people sat in a circle. He turned his guilty eyes away from theirs and paced through the room, remembering to take a right turn into the kitchen.

His sweet old Irish Nan sat at a dining table, oblivious to his arrival.

Between sips of tea, she watched him with the same scared eyes as everyone else, until all at once, her face unravelled with a mischievous grin.

"Ooo it's Le-ee-on. What have you been doing with yourself today now?" she asked like she always had.

"Just taking it easy," he lied.

"Well, you deserve it now Leon. Here would you like one of these cakes?" she said. And like a magician sprang a chocolate muffin under his nose.

"Yes please," said Leon, placing the cake on the table. He had learned long ago that whether he wanted it or not was irrelevant. So to distract her from his crime, Leon moved the chat along, saying, "Do you like it here?"

"Oh yes, the people here are lovely. Apart from 'Fanny Malone' over there," she yelled, pointing to the back of an egg shaped lady across the room.

"Well I'm glad you're enjoying it," he broke into laughter.

Her filter was gone - if she ever even had one, he thought.

"I had to tell off two girls last night though," she said jumping thoughts, "I said you expect me to look after you and you're coming back at one o'clock in the morning on a school night. So I gave them a good telling off and sent them to bed. But now they know not to do it again now see."

He judged her straight face and crossed eyebrows and decided she must have been serious - talking about the nurses instead, most likely.

"Oh watch out for old Fanny Malone," she yelled again. Except this time it wasn't funny. As she clenched her jaw rock tight and hissed between the cracks of her lips.

The rotund lady had begun waddling toward them, but she only needed to come within five feet for his Nan to yell, "Ahhh," like a banshee. Clearly used to it, the fellow old timer walked past without even flinching.

What is this crazy town? He thought.

"It's okay she's fine," said Leon, "I'm going to take you

to your hospital appointment now," he changed the subject.

"Oh is it today is it? Well hold on now, let me get ready."

The words came out as the plaid jacket went on, but her hands flailed for something else.

"Oh but where's my scarf?" she panicked, "I've lost my scarf can you find it?"

He could see exactly where she left it, saying, "Check your pocket."

"Oh, there it is. Whatever would I do without you now Leon?"

She grinned with a crumb of cake giving her piano teeth and he smiled back. The clearest form of communication. Most importantly enough to calm her, as Leon lead his Nan out of the home and into the street.

"Is this a new car you have?" she said, pointing to the Civic.

"Yeah, do you like it?"

"Oh yes, it's very nice."

He opened the car door and she fell across two seats, saying, "Come sit beside me now Leon."

"But who's going to drive?"

"Quick before the bus goes."

Interested to see how this version of events played out, he got in the back as commanded, and waited for the next improv cue.

"Good boy Leon," she said and patted him on the head, like she used to do, for her dog Ralph. This was one scene he was absolutely not playing out.

"Okay I'm going to go drive now," said Leon.

Clutch. Ignition. And far away.

"Oh the ride is moving," she yelled.

He drove like he was trying to escape her in the back. Because being with family felt like a different time. Forgotten for good reason, and felt deeply when her grin in the mirror made him feel like a little boy. He had gone a while without this strange guilt, and the *18 mins* did not go quickly.

"Where are we going? How long until we get there? Where are we going?" she peppered him. Until eventually, they arrived beneath the hospital. The silver building glistened far above their small bodies, encircling Leon's periphery.

He shut the door behind his grandma, and she followed him like a shadow into the hospital. They took the escalator to *level 1* and the elevator to *3*, walking down wide corridors on shiny floors.

"Do you smell that?" she asked excited, "Someone's done a good job cleaning."

They stood outside of an airtight door more familiar to Leon in Sci-fi movies, and he pressed a big green button below the sign *Orange Unit*. Ten seconds. One minute. They waited, with Leon watching the empty box window of the door. When it felt like forever had passed, a finger like ET's crept across the window and the cylinders in the lock un-sprung. Finally, Leon opened the door, seeing only the back of a nurse marching away – his usual sight of them.

"Well you never know do you, I mean it could be

anything, you never know, I know," squealed a nasal voice.

The howling came from the lady sat at Reception, chatting on her cell phone. Her uneven face caught Leon's attention. With eyes like a frog and ticks drawn on above them she chortled through her nose, twiddling hair which reminded Leon of an old carpet he had. But she was happy, and I need to stop judging people, he thought.

"Are you waiting?" she asked.

"Yes we're here to see Dr Radford," he replied.

"Take a seat please."

"Have a seat Nan," he said.

"Oh okay then."

They sat on their favourite row of plastic seats. Back inside the white wonderland. Ready to pretend there was a happy ending.

"Hello Mrs Fields," called the voice of Dr Radford.

Out of any number of corridors he appeared, arms out like a preacher, clapping his hands.

"Good to see you, Mrs Fields, how are you feeling?" he practically sang.

"Ha ha, I am great thank you Doctor and yourself?" she responded with joy.

"Wonderful. Can I borrow you for five minutes?"

Dr Radford extended his hand to her.

"Oh I have to stay with Leon here now," she said turning between them confused.

"I'll be right here waiting. You go," said Leon.

"Ha ha okay then - you stay right here then."

Down the far corridor she toddled, behind the Dr and out of sight. Out of mind.

Leon lay his head back on the wall and closed his eyes. Only for the room's silence to be interrupted by someone sitting in front of him. They moved restless, through fluttering breaths, and he listened curiously.

She sat with her head bowed, arms folded and her knees pointed inward. Uncooperative to the world around her. Yet the centre reference to which the room fit, posing like a sad portrait, while the world denied her sadness. Rays shone through the window pane and fell down her dusky hair, on splintered ends laying on sun kissed skin. Three times her black fingernails tugged on the sleeve of a denim jacket, grazing clenched fists on a black mini skirt. Her breaths began to slow.

From under ruffled bangs, she looked up at him by accident. Deliberately, slowly, she crept her eyes towards him again, and he was still watching.

"So what are you here for?" he asked.

Her mouth fumbled the word, "huh," while her head returned to the default tilt. Surprised to be talked to, she started again, "The kind of things I don't talk about with strangers," she said bluntly.

"A doctor is a stranger."

"True," she fake laughed, half-hearted.

They lifted their heads together and Leon saw her clearly: no older than twenty five, Italian maybe. Her lips full and pouted, her nose short and buttoned. Thinly arched eyebrows rose mockingly as she looked right through him. And into sky blue eyes he caught his reflection, staring like a little boy again. She reminded him of no one.

"Okay pop quiz to speed up this awkward encounter," she continued, "do you ever feel like you're not really here? Like you wake up in the middle of a conversation, thinking, shit this is actually real?"

"That's quite specific," he said, enjoying how out there it was.

"Yeah, I'm weird let's deal with it."

"Every Sunday morning after a heavy night out," said Leon, "so that doesn't sound so different to me, is that why you're here?"

"Yeah-well-no it's more complicated than that, obviously," she protested, and decided the best evasive action was a different question, "so, what are you depressed about?"

"I'm not."

"Really you look depressed," she said spitefully. Though quickly embarrassed at herself, as she rolled her eyes away.

Leon doubled-down and smiled, saying, "Really?"

"Yeah you smile too much, no one is actually that happy. But why *are* you here?"

"For my grandma."

"So she's depressed?"

"She has Dementia."

"Oh I'm sorry," her voice lowered on each letter.

"It's fine."

She motioned to speak but quit so Leon jumped in,

saying, "You know joking aside I have felt similar to you, and long story short I should have come somewhere like this, I think you'll be alright here."

"Oh spare me the preaching, please," she leapt on his words.

"I did I just skipped to the end."

"As simple as that yeah?"

"Yeah, I also have a Jehovah's witness pamphlet if you'd like it."

She was ready to bite back but froze at his punchline. She didn't know if he was actually joking until he started laughing too.

"Oh ha ha," she said, "but you still don't know me."

"No I don't," he smiled to her, "but you'll see."

"Yes I'll be glad to disappoint you."

Before she could decide if his smile was creepy or cute, office 6 along the corridor opened with a clang, and Dr Radford stepped out scoping the room. His sights stopped at the back of Leon's new friend.

"Ellie Antonova," called the Dr.

"That's me," she told Leon.

"See you around, Ellie."

"Yeah," said Ellie as she strutted away.

Mid-step and halfway towards the door she turned back to Leon. And with her arms raised to the walls said, "You know where to find me."

"Erm, Leon," announced Dr Radford, "give me one second Ellie."

He came over holding a business card with some scribble on it.

"Take this, I've written an address on the back for you. Normally it's just the patients who go to this meeting," he shrugged, "it's like a free space for them to meet others, open up and ask questions. But I think it would be better if you came in place of your grandma."

"Thanks," Leon said unsure.

"Okay great, and if you need me, my contact details are on the front. Your grandma is just with a nurse now but she'll be out in a minute."

6pm, tomorrow night. Kings Hall (two streets down from the hospital), read sloppy hand writing on the American Psycho like card. But he was still thinking about Ellie.

INSIDE STORY

Cereal crumbs tumbled down Max's uniform as she slipped into sleep. Back hunched, head first she drifted out of the office chair. Back on the job, chasing Leon once more behind her eyes. Only to feel like she missed a step, falling back awake, as she slid off the seat.

She played with her flyaway hair and didn't notice the mess with her eyes still closed. An inch to the right, an inch to the left, she fidgeted her skinny ass to find the right spot again, boots crossed on the desk.

Last month's car chase replayed, the first real action she'd had as a detective. She twitched as she dreamt, rocking with the vehicle, except this time she was the one fleeing, and as fast as Max tried, she could not escape.

Thirty six hours since she'd been home, Max was makeup free, still in the same smelly clothes and out of fucks. A proud Latina woman, who had enough inappropriate compliments on her looks to enjoy being a so-called mess.

Like the worst alarm clock in the world, a vacuum launched into action across the room. The little circular machine hovered towards her, and Max's foot was ready to smash it like a hockey puck.

"Do not kick my vacuum, Alvarez."

The Chief's motherly voice played over the police station's speakers.

"What the fuck," she whispered.

"Language, Max. There are worse ways I could wake you up."

"Umm Chief, are you watching me on the surveillance?" she protested.

"I'm not a fan of early morning TV, so yeah. And can you not always sleep on the job please."

"What do you mean?" said Max playing dumb.

"I mean metaphorically and literally."

"Maybe I was pondering a case."

"Great, let me come through and talk about," the speaker faded out.

Chief McCormack's heavy footsteps travelled along the corridor while Max tried to sort herself out, fixing her tie and checking her breath for alcohol.

"Whatever," she gave up.

The Chief was an old timer, in her attitude as much as her age. Nobody asked how old she was, but her stories of the Gulf War gave a hint. The fact she was ex-military always got the young recruits whispering. She wasn't an imposing size, average height and stout, still she had a march which sounded like the North Korean troops. Max saw her a little differently than most though, like Chief's cute 'blowfish' cheeks she told people, rounded off by her can-I-speak-to-the-manager-please bob cut. There was also Chief's phlegmatic expression. Was she angry? Was she sad? To Max, she was like a mother figure. A half Irish Caucasian mother figure who was nothing like her, but more caring than her own family.

With a face like a spanked owl Chief entered the office, and for once Max knew she was angry today.

Chief switched off the vacuum, saying, "Why are you here so early this week?"

"Alicia kicked me out."

"Again?" hooted Chief.

"For good this time, apparently."

"I'm sorry to hear that Max."

"Me too," she said.

"You aren't sleeping here at night are you?"

"Oh hell no Chief," Max pretended everything was okay, "I just don't like waking up in hotels."

"What can you tell me about the disappearance of Heather Dodd?" said Chief.

"We," she coughed to buy time, "nothing concrete Ma'am. We checked out her last known location at the nightclub Opium, but we don't have any standout suspects on the CCTV. She left the club alone at 4AM."

"Have you checked her phone records? Or taxi cameras?"

"We're awaiting results this morning Ma'am."

"But you do have suspects right?" Chief became agitated.

"We're rounding them up."

"Good. I want daily updates on this," Chief patted

Max's shoulder, "and I've told you about ironing your shirt."

Chief left Max sweeping cereal crumbs off her crumpled shirt, and with a quick fix of her ponytail too she was ready – at least for the morning rabble.

"And then I shouted, don't move. The kid jumped three feet in the air and landed on his hip. I hear the crack, he's screaming, it's 100% broke. Next thing I know I've got all the local moms coming out of their houses, yelling at me for assaulting a twelve year old. Horrific," said Joe Schembri.

Max avoided eye contact, after Joe asked her out last week and she had to awkwardly explain her 'boyfriend' was called Alicia.

She felt a hand on her shoulder too strong to be the Chief's, and saw the giant dark hand of her partner, Denzel.

"Wakey, wakey, rise and shine," Denzel bellowed.

"I'm ready."

"Well you look like shit," Denzel revelled in his immaculate suit, never complete without a tie clip. 6'5" with limbs like tree trunks, a heart of gold and a face out of a kid's nightmare. Maybe Max wasn't ready to wake up yet.

"Have we had any response for witnesses?" Denzel's voice had so much bass it was like being interrogated by Barry White, "For Heather Dodd's disappearance?" he added.

"Sorry no, nothing yet."

"Alright, well I've got something for you," Denzel

pulled up a chair beside her, "do you remember the guy we lost in the car chase last month?"

"I was thinking about it just this morning," Max sat up.

"Check this. The car is a match for the Los Muertos killings."

"The Cartel members?" Max's words jumped.

"You got it. I knew something was all wrong about that guy. You remember the case right?"

"Only on the news," said Max.

"Well here's the real inside story. A friend from the academy works for the DEA, Frank Lynch. They got a tip on a courier of the Los Muertos' cocaine. They follow it to La Cabellera, Mexico. They're told to follow a black 2013 Chevrolet Camaro to a chicken farm – the same car our new friend is driving. But they never find it. The informant buckles and gives them the farm's location. Frank storms the spot without even a warrant. What does he find?"

Max wasn't sure if this was a real question.

"Flies celebrating three Cartel members dead. Including the Los Muertos Cartel's top hitman, Cezar 'The Hammer' Rodriguez. All three had shotgun wounds, they close off the area for forensics. Our buddy Frank is driving back to the police station, when these half naked kids start running across the road. Where'd they come from? The chicken farm, they say."

"Right it was a trafficking ring as well," said Max.

"Right," said Denzel, "but what they didn't tell you in the news is the kids say a white guy in the black

Camaro drove them away."

"After killing the Cartel members?" Max's voice broke.

"Or maybe our friend just escaped with the kids. Who knows?"

"Well let's find out," Max got excited.

"In good time. We have plenty of other cases right now, don't you forget."

"But wait surely there's a lot of 2013 black Chevrolet Camaros?"

They paused to consider the notion. Max was just pretending to think, actually shitting herself at having a missing teenage girl and a case involving a Mexican drug cartel in her first few months as a detective.

"Oh did I not mention the informant gave us the licence plate too?" asked Denzel innocently.

"You're terrible at telling stories."

"How do you think the car showed up on our records?"

"But he hasn't even changed the license plate, really?" asked Max, "it's like he wants to be caught."

FORGETTING ABOUT EVERYTHING ELSE

7th MAY

"Seriously how long are these corridors?" Jean shouted.

"I can't be turning up late, I organised the damn thing," Dr Radford had his own conversation.

They made a hullabaloo, looking like the Ministry of Silly Walks.

"I told you we needed to leave earlier for the traffic," he said.

"You're messing up your shirt running like that."

He acted like he didn't hear her and powered on.

"Just take anything you miss off the counsellor's notes, it's pretty much his show tonight anyway," Jean added.

"I know," he said, blowing out nerves.

He broke on his heels at the hall's entrance, remembering to wipe the sweat from his forehead but forgot about the shirt. The panic bolt door slammed behind them, as they tip-toed around people's seats, falling into the odd waltz. Two empty folding chairs finally arrived at the end of the row, behind columns of people.

"How's it going?" whispered Dr Radford.

"You haven't missed much of interest," mumbled the monotone Counsellor beside him.

The hall was silent for the speaker…

"Suicide is a full term solution to a short term problem."

The speaker's cap cast gloom over his face, on sullen eyes scattering over the audience, onto Leon. A bead of sweat ran down his black skin and fell onto the reading stand.

"I say these words, and they make sense. And I take a step back from the bridge. I say these words every day, until eventually, they're just words again, and I'm still broke with four kids."

The audience remained mute but for singular coughs and dragging chairs. Leon watched the 'thug from the hood' be ignored and felt on his side.

"You can't reason with yourself if you're crazy. And if you're not crazy and you want to kill yourself, well there was probably a damn good reason for it."

What a sad room, thought Leon taking a look around. All caught up in themselves. He sat right in the middle of the odd crowd and turned to observe those along his row. They watched the speaker gormlessly, but maybe they were bored because he was only saying what they already knew.

"My name is Josh Morgan, and I'm here for my family."

The speaker lumbered off the stage to subdued applause.

Beneath the dingy yellow lights, in a sticky and uncomfortably packed hall, Leon was ready to leave - until Dr Radford took the stage. With a warm smile, he said, "Why are so many of our younger generation depressed?" The question filled the room without an answer.

"You might think you would be content. Since you are accused of being focused on your social lives, narcissists, and determined to take the easy route. You are the Millennial, Gen Z or whatever name they come up with next to group together anyone under forty. I guess the better question is what do you really want in life? Is it to take it easy? Or is it actually to have a purposeful impact? Either way, it doesn't seem people are very happy about their options, whether it be in relationships, jobs or our living environment. So what is the missing piece? Is it your parent's fault? Maybe you were told you could have anything you wanted in life? I remember telling my child she could be anything she wanted, not that she would be."

The words felt personal to Dr Radford, but Leon heard them like they were his own.

"I speak to a lot of you, and I guess the trouble is,

the options don't even seem there for you anymore. Apart from which filter to place onto your life. But are we really going to blame social media? To be fair, it didn't feel good to be unfriended or blocked right? Oh, I haven't mentioned Tinder or Netflix yet," he paused, "that's because they're not that important, and I think you know it, actually. A lot of you tell me about real life problems, like Josh who bravely just told us about his fight to provide for his family. Or some of you who are victims of serious crimes. In truth, I believe a lot of you do have the right perspective, but many of you are missing approval, not least from my generation, which is lazy in its labelling. And sometimes from yourselves. This lack of approval can lead to a loss of self-worth. Filling the void is loneliness, substance abuse and suicide. So what next? There isn't an app for all our problems, yet, and the longer we ponder the issues of your generation, the more wealth disparity grows in this country.

The first step is to not blame yourselves. Please. We can all climb up the mountain together, giving each other a push, we can go a lot further than being alone. Make valuable connections by starting with a simple conversation tonight. Whether on this microphone or to the person next to you. Remove the filter and be real with each other about your problems. Because if we all have problems, are they as bad as we think inside our own minds?" Dr Radford paused to feel the room.

"Can I eat yet?" shouted Donnie from the back, provoking hisses and laughter in equal measure.

Dr Radford sighed into the microphone, "Thank you

for your input Donnie, we usually wait a little longer but sure it's about dinner time so we'll break here for ten minutes. There are also drinks at the back of the hall on the far side, thank you."

The chair legs dragged back on the floor, overlapping the Dr's words, and everybody walked away. Except for Leon, who sat where he was, observing. He found Ellie in the crowd of people, spinning around in circles, lost at sea in a queue for salmon. Her face without makeup, hair in a bun, she appeared comfortable in a baggy LA Lakers hoody, and still out of place. The crowd chatted amongst themselves, but Ellie just watched the backs of heads. The queue moved at zombie pace, apart from the Dr, who jumped from platter to platter, filling his plate with sandwiches. Leon made his way over to him, saying, "Is it always this cheery?"

Dr Radford turned around with his mouth wedged with food and looking guilty, but he relaxed when he realised it was Leon.

"Oo-you-jus-wait-till-da-encore," Dr Radford mumbled through chews, "ha, ha I joke. But not really - it's always like this. But it is helpful for us. Have you tried thee-"

"So why am I here?" asked Leon.

"Well…" Dr Radford finally swallowed his food and explained, "Doctor Hauser is going to clarify the next steps of the process in just a moment, which may be of greater benefit to yourself. But I hope you keep coming to these sessions Leon, to act as a go between for us and for your grandma... Plus, it's nice just to be around another normal person," he whispered and jokingly made a shush sign.

"Don't worry Doc, I got you."

"Call me Robert, and see you around kid."

Leon threw him a lazy salute, and Dr Radford carried his plates away.

Ellie meandered at the buffet table beside Leon, picking pieces of food and dropping them.

"Don't take it out on the sausage rolls," Leon said behind her. Ellie didn't turn around or say anything, but then she recognised his voice.

"It's you," Ellie recited with pretend surprise, "you aren't following me are you?"

"Well you did tell me where to find you."

"I suppose I'll take some of the blame then. But I wouldn't recommend this as the place to be."

"But seriously, does it help you though? Talking and hearing about it?" asked Leon

"Did you hear the speeches in there?" Ellie asked rhetorically.

They laughed in time with each other.

"Any more and I'm going to need the tissues from my car," joked Leon, "so I'm going to leave as soon as the pizza table is free."

"Why are you here anyway?"

"Just to pick up information for my grandma, apparently."

To dodge the subject Ellie spun around with her eyes still on Leon, "I think I'm going to leave too," she said with her face pretending to think.

"I'll walk you out," he said.

Ellie motioned to speak, but didn't, and walked on ahead with her arms crossed. She contemplated turning down the offer, but there was something about Leon she found attractive. Aside from looking like all her bad exes, Leon was different because he knew who he was.

They walked down quiet hallways beside each other, waiting for the other person to speak.

"Did you mean what you said the other day?" Ellie said suddenly.

"Which part?"

"When you said I would be alright."

"Of course," said Leon.

"Why?"

"Because you're a Lakers fan, you're a glutton for pain."

"Fuck off," Ellie broke out in laughter, "and who do you support?"

"Oh for my sins, the Lakers too."

Ellie turned to Leon and held his shoulder like she was about to give big news, "Well, there might just be hope for you too Leon."

"Enough to go on a date with me?"

Ellie stopped in her tracks.

"It's not fair to say these things to me," she pleaded, "stop it."

"Okay," Leon brushed it off.

"Okay then," she said tentatively.

Face to face they studied each other, eyes locked and laughing nervously. Their acting was over, and they let themselves be genuinely happy, at least for this moment. And it was too late to be nervous now decided Ellie. She leant forward and he kissed her - but not for long enough thought Leon, as Ellie pulled away.

"Let's get coffee or something tomorrow?" he asked.

"Coffee?" laughed Ellie mockingly.

"Or shots, whatever," he joked.

"Okay sure - we'll get coffee. If people actually still do that."

"Do you have your phone?"

Ellie took out her cell and Leon saved his number on the phone, making sure to call himself too, ensuring the digits were correct.

"Well, I better be going I guess – yep," Ellie confirmed to herself awkwardly, nodding, smiling, stepping away with her hands in her pockets.

This girl is something, thought Leon.

"See you tomorrow," he shouted down the hallway, trying to make her turn around.

"Coffee," Ellie beamed over her shoulder.

Leon let the seconds pass watching her walk away, forgetting about everything else.

MAD DREAMS

Wild lights danced in the dark, red, blue and
white

As stars fell like dandelions in spring

His mad dreams fought with waking life tonight

Four notes. Sixteen beats. The loud and beeping ring-
tone awoke Leon from his sleep. He reached across to
his bedside table and grabbed the light. *Vincent* read
the dialling name. "Hello," he answered.

"You gotta come get me man," Vincent screamed,
"I'm dying."

"What?"

"I said come get me, I'm fucking dying, I need your
help."

"Where?"

"Fashion District off Olympic Boulevard, some-some-

some side street. I'm bleeding out man," Vincent's words shivered in pain.

"I'll be five minutes."

Leon threw on any clothes scattered around him, flew down the stairs and leapt into the car in a hot minute. The tyres echoed Vincent's screams as he sped out onto the streets. He slid between angry traffic, skating the car across the road and drifting around bends. He was on auto-pilot and ignoring the noise in a silent panic. Vincent sounded convincing.

Leon slowed as he drew near the Fashion District, approaching below a rising hill he could see nothing over the road's horizon. The sound of his ticking engine spread out without reply. *04:16*. Leon was already five minutes late. He climbed over the hill but still nothing. Trapped between the towers, he felt more like the hunted than the searcher, a sitting duck in an open stream. Each alleyway and gap in the street was visible only in the shapes of its shadows.

Wait, hit Leon's thoughts like lightning. He rolled back and saw the silhouette of a body sat against an alley wall. Engine on, he jumped out of the car. The body remained only a figure until he knelt down beside it and turned his head. It was Vincent. What was left of him. Leon felt a gash on the back of Vincent's head and looked into eyes swollen shut. He began to lift him but slipped - Leon was kneeling in a pool of blood, running not from Vincent's head, but somewhere else altogether: Vincent's leg was gone. Severed below the knee cap.

Fuck, no time to sit here, thought Leon. He took off his jacket and t-shirt and tied them around the stump, hurling Vincent's limp body over his shoulders, when he heard a metal clang. The noise came from around a corner further down the alley. Leon delicately placed Vincent back down and crept towards the sound. Within each flicker of his eyelids the corner merged between shades of black. As he stepped closer to the edge, he kept his back against the wall, hands raised. His senses roared, to the sound of the beating engine, which grew faster with his heart - to the blood which seeped down his face, dripping onto his bare chest - to the corner. Leon jumped out ready for violence, but only emptiness stared back at him.

He retraced his steps carefully, keeping his eyes fixed at the core of the darkness. No time for this, he thought, speeding back to Vincent. Over his shoulders Leon hurled Vincent's body again, now convulsing, and frantically laid him in the car's passenger seat. He raced against Vincent's slowing breaths to the hospital, checking his pulse each minute. But he did not try and wake him to this nightmare. Leon skid the car around the hospital parking lot to its entrance, braking heavily behind a man who leapt in fright.

"Hey please," Leon shouted, "I need help."

The old boy froze in shock.

Leon sprang out of the vehicle and slung open the passenger door.

"I said I need help," he shouted again, dragging Vincent by his armpits until help finally arrived. The two of them carried Vincent toward the hospital with Leon turning his face from the Samaritan, wary of being identified.

"I dropped this guy's wallet and I.D. you bring him in I'm getting it," Leon said leaving Vincent in the strangers arms.

"What?" yelped the helper.

"Get him in there right *now*, I'll be one minute."

Vincent hung in the man's arms like meat on a rail, and Leon walked away. Unable to turn back, he carried on into the night, wondering if he had just been a pall-bearer for his best friend.

ELEPHANT IN
THE ROOM

Fresh sunlight broke in the morning clouds, riding gusts of wind down to a lonesome tree. Ellie sat inside the busy coffee shop *Estella's,* watching the branches sweep from side to side through the window. Groups gathered along the street for lunch, laughing, tweeting, kicking the swirling leaves down the path. None stopping Ellie's daydream, or rather, her anxiety.

Her body faced the shop's entrance, her head elsewhere. She twiddled her thumbs, switching her gaze between the street and the door, smiling awkwardly at the waitress as she passed. Ellie bit her chapped lips and read her inner forearm: *I walk in your memory.* It was for her mother, and the only tattoo she cared to have.

She cared a little about this date too, failing miserably to treat it casually. She'd even made the effort to wear makeup for once. Still, Ellie didn't want to seem too keen, so she put her hair in a ponytail and threw on a white tee and denim jeans. Tightly fitted though, with her white ballet flats, as he was 6ft and she was 5ft9 already. Sometimes she would overthink things, even when Ellie knew they didn't really matter.

Somehow surprised to see Leon turn up for their arranged date, she spotted him crossing the road towards the coffee shop. Phone off the table – sit upright, ready, she thought, rattling her fingers along the table top. The squeaky sound of the door opening was clear, but she waited until his footsteps were beside her, before turning to say, "Hi," startled and cheery.

"Good morning," said Leon, taking the seat right next to her, "have you ordered?"

"No-no, I was waiting for you."

Leon had not taken as much care when getting ready. He showered until his skin was wrinkled, burned his bloody clothes in the forest, and wore a brand new leather bike jacket like it was just another date. Except dried blood was stuck under his fingernails. Beneath the table he tried to scratch the blood away without looking down again, keeping his face calm and smiley. Ellie returned the gesture, but was not as good at pretending to be comfortable, so, Leon tried to break the silence, saying, "What have you been up to then?"

"Oh, today? Erm, nothing really. I just slept in, watched this dog skate on Instagram, sung with The Weeknd in the shower, the usual stuff, you?"

Leon remembered carrying Vincent's convulsing body.

"Yeah, pretty much the same here."

No one said anything for five awkward seconds.

"So how long have you lived here?" Ellie asked.

"I was born here, but I've just come back after a few years away. How about you?"

"Lived here all my life. But I always dreamt of getting away," she confessed, "where did you travel to?"

Leon could not answer Ellie with specifics, simply because he would need to lie. And from experience, he knew these lies would snowball and crush any trust they had in the future.

"Up and down the West Coast, a little bit of Mexico."

"Oh? Exciting," exclaimed Ellie, waiting for Leon to elaborate. He did not. Silence returned and dragged them down in their seats. Ellie's shoulders hung disappointed, and her eyes slipped to staring at the sugar shaker on the table. How can I be such an idiot? He thought.

"What can I get you?" interrupted an overly happy teenage waitress, all freckles and braces.

Ellie jumped up at the chance to start a conversation, "Yes please, a large latte please," she said.

"And for you sir?"

"A small Americano, thank you," said Leon.

"Coming right up."

"Are you in a rush?" asked Ellie.

"Not at all, just planning on doing more talking than drinking."

"Well, you better get talking then," half-joked Ellie, and they laughed together at the elephant in the room.

"I'm sorry," said Leon, "remember you said sometimes you wake up wondering what's real?"

"Of course," said Ellie, "something like that."

"Well last night was a nightmare for me, and I keep remembering I wasn't dreaming. I woke up to an emergency call from my friend around 4AM and had to drive him to the hospital."

"Oh shit," dropped Ellie's jaw, "are they going to be okay?"

"Yeah fine," lied Leon, "he had a car accident and the vehicle was too totalled for him to drive, he was shaken up but thankfully no one was hurt too bad."

"And you still made it to our date?" beamed Ellie.

"Of course," said Leon.

"Wow you must really like coffee," she said coy.

"Something like that," he copied her.

"But that's probably the least fun first date story ever told," Leon realised, "so let's talk more about you."

"Sure," said Ellie with an upper infliction, "though in case you haven't noticed, my life isn't all sunshine and rainbows either," she laughed.

"But how are you now?"

"Well apart from my immediate hatred for that phrase, I actually feel slightly better. I mean, it was pretty depressing at the meeting last night. But this morning it's been nice to only worry about which clothes I should wear to our date. Which is a nice change, and I guess we can thank you a little for that, but don't smile," Ellie pointed at him, with her serious face melting into a grin.

"I'm not," promised Leon, with fingers over his

twitching mouth.

"I used to just tell my mom all of this stuff instead, so we can also thank her for my over-sharing," said Ellie.

"Where is she now?"

"She's enjoying her early retirement on the East Coast, we still talk now and then so it's cool."

"Lucky woman," said Leon.

"That was a lie I'm sorry. My mother died a long time ago."

"Okay," answered Leon calmly but confused.

"It's just a habit I have to lie about things I would rather not talk about."

"Oh, I understand perfectly," he said from years of experience.

"But I don't want to start off lying to you."

"And the truth always comes out eventually," he added.

"Okay detective," said Ellie cheekily. Leon got distracted by dimples when she smiled. It was silly, like their conversations, but all of it was natural, "By the way, what's your job, if you don't mind me asking?"

Leon held Ellie's hand, and staring into her eyes softly, said, "I'm an astronaut."

"No you're not," she giggled but accidentally snorted, "ignore that."

"Okay I'm not an astronaut that was my one lie to you."

"I should hope so too because we can't both be lying all the time."

"I guess we'll have to spend more time together practising being normal," he said.

"I'd like that," she said holding his hand a little tighter.

Their bubble was burst by the crashing of a tray full of glasses and juices spilling towards them. Leon was back kneeling in a pool of Vincent's blood.

"I've enjoyed seeing you again, but I need to go for now," he said.

"You really are in a rush."

"Not by my choice, I promise. It's about last night."

"Oh go-go, your friend is more important right now," she protested, "and let me know how it goes."

"Deal," said Leon, and she followed his lead to a kiss.

Leon left the café and watched Ellie finish her coffee from inside his car across the street. This was a window he wanted to keep open, and he meant what he told her. He just hoped his promise to see her again wasn't a lie. The window wipers swept the leaves back into the swirling sky and he threw caution to the wind, driving into the growing storm hoping for change like a sad cliché but happy all the same.

NOT DEAD YET

"Did you remember to change his IV?" asked a doctor officiously.

"Yes half an hour ago," answered the nurse.

Their voices were timbers below the beeping heart monitor, and Leon listened to every sound, waiting outside the hospital room. Vincent lay on the bed, bandaged like a mummy about to meet the daddy of all hangovers. His limbs were sprawled across the sheets, at least what remained of his right leg stump, staining the bandages in blackened blood.

The patchwork continued up to his head, with two purple clams for eyes, on perished yellow skin which putrefied the warm air. Inhale – exhale, his heavy breaths echoed within the oxygen mask, in rhythm to the heart monitor, playing the percussion. Cables entangled his body, pumping drugs into his veins - the first substances ever injected for his health. He remained unconscious to the horror victim he had become.

"His vitals have stabled, but we're not out of the woods yet," said a doctor, "check on him every half hour please. Now, for the case of Mr Jones, come walk with me, please."

As they drew nearer to Leon behind the door, he drifted into an adjacent room, hiding in the dark with other sleeping patients. Until their footsteps faded out and he emerged from the shadows back to the door's window, deciding it was time to say hello.

Without making a noise Leon stood beneath a glaring spotlight over Vincent, tempted to scare him, despite the circumstance. Vincent looked even worse up close. He kept tapping his hand on Vincent's sweaty cheek, but no one was home. The tap turned into a mini slap. Voila, thought Leon, as Vincent's eyes rolled like marbles, stopping as his pupils focused on Leon. Jolted by reality, he gasped for air.

"So you're not dead yet?" asked Leon deadpan.

Vincent groaned in pain and confusion.

"Okay, maybe you're a little dead."

More unintelligible words were uttered beneath the oxygen mask, so Leon took it off.

"Fuck you," croaked Vincent.

"What happened?" asked Leon.

"We were ambushed."

Leon took a cup of water from the side tray and poured it into Vincent's dry mouth.

"Why?" said Leon.

"I don't fucking know," Vincent strained, spluttering, "I was doing the job, the one I offered you, transporting the coke. Why not? Easy money right. We passed all the hot spots. We're on the home straight, nobody was even in sight. Maybe I got lazy. More water please?"

Leon held his neck like a baby and poured. Vincent's gaze got lost in the spotlight.

"But next thing I know a car hits the front of the vehicle, and another the back. Just gunshots everywhere. Sounded like automatics. Flying through the walls like rain. The other two guys held onto the shelves of the van when we were hit, and the bullets splashed through them. I'd fallen over when we crashed. I laid there like a bitch with my hands over my head until they dragged me out...

I didn't even reach for my gun, as far as I was concerned I was already dead. They just laughed at me and took turns stamping. I was barely conscious, just staring up at blurred colours. But I remember one prick saying, if you want to live you're gonna have to bleed for it. It was the worst pain I ever felt. My thigh pulsed like It was going to explode, and I knew the rest was gone. I looked up at his face, and I'll never forget it, the cunt is just smiling like its Christmas. Now get crawling, he says. I tried but I passed out quickly, woke up I don't know when and that's when I called you. I thought I was going to die, man, you know?" he cried, "The fucking freaks didn't even wear masks. I mean, what the fuck? What the fuck are we even dealing with here?" Vincent faltered to a whisper.

"We're going to find out," Leon promised.

"Shit, I can't do anything ever again. Fuck all left of me," Vincent began to sob. His raging tears rived open a cut below his eye, running through the blood.

"We'll get you a new leg, a badass robotic one," said Leon, "and who knows, it might even give you a better gangsta limp."

A laugh slipped through his grimacing.

"You're alive and you'll make it back."

"If I do I tell you something," said Vincent grinding teeth, grappling the rail of his bed, "I'm gonna get him if it's the last thing I ever do."

Vincent's veins pulsated with fury, conducting the medical instruments to a fever pitch. Leon realised that no robotic leg or amount of time would heal Vincent's pain, or stop him from getting into more trouble. He would have to be the one to orchestrate the hunt for his attackers.

A CAVE OF
BUTTERFLIES

His mind was a cave of dark thoughts, holding on to his daughter's butterfly.

She handed him the vibrant creature in their home garden, its broken wings shimmering shades of black and blue under the sun. A distant memory, giving way to fluttering voices. A thousand of them, all around.

Dr Radford watched people pass him by in the shopping mall, sitting in the comfortable armchair of his favourite coffee shop, *The Old Bridge*. Families with children, youngsters on dates, they swarmed in a rush up and down the shopping mall. Two teenagers caught his eye, walking hand in hand. The boy had a mop on his head like the old mods of Dr Radford's youth, milky skin, chipmunk cheeks and awkward movements, but being beside the girl made him walk on air. She was a few inches taller, and also made his Pink Floyd t-shirt and jeans look scruffy in her flowing forget-me-not dress. The girl swept golden blonde hair behind her ear and smiled carefree with a mouth full of metal.

The truth is she reminded the Dr of his daughter, and how he imagined her lost teenage years. So he swiftly abandoned half a cup of coffee in the empty terrace of the shop, and regrettably joined the swarm, standing in line down an escalator, when a foot kicked him in the back.

"Sorry," a woman repented, "no Jordan naughty, don't kick the man."

Dr Radford didn't even turn around, he just waited for his turn to get off, and when it came wistfully strolled into the newsagents.

VALENTINE'S DAY/ANNIVERSARY/*MOTIVATIONAL* - his eyes paused at the last card category and read them out of curiosity.

Your Only Limit Is You

Your Flaws Are Perfect for the Heart That Is Meant to Love You

Whatever Is Meant to Be Will Always Find a Way

"Bullshit," he retorted, "clichés that ignore hard truths, statements that justify selfish mistakes," he muttered, "and a cynical appropriation of peoples hope, that leaves them blind to the real obstacles of their lives," he began to shout, "but I suppose hope is just another product to sell, don't question the real issues," Dr Radford broke out in jazz hands, "the age old ploy by the profiteers of the status quo."

He checked himself before he went full on crazy old guy in public, but thankfully only books had caught his outburst. His eyes rolled onto the card category he wanted: *BIRTHDAYS.*

Happy Birthday Son, May Your Dreams Come True

Happy Birthday My Darling Daughter

To My Wife With Love

He paid for the latter in a rush, leaving the store with Jean's birthday card stashed in his Mac jacket pocket. In zig-zags, he staggered between the bodies flowing toward him, with light from the atrium making him more long sighted than usual.

Four hours he'd been sitting in the café but he didn't feel ready to go home. He reached the parking lot under thick pelting rain, with the rainbow seeming a bit ironic. He fell into his Range Rover SUV and took a moment to watch the shower hit the windshield, happy to be back within his own four walls. As slow as the clouds he drove home, intending to go there only for a minute, before driving to *O'Grady's*, just for one beer, maybe.

He pushed open the familiar creaking door of the bar, and was greeted by damp air and the sound of Prince's Purple Rain. The place was empty but for the bartender, a fat bald man with goblin features and ragged black beard. Or 'Gerry' as Dr Radford knew him. He wiped down the bar's top with a washcloth, merrily spilling water off it and onto his vest as he went.

"Here he is," welcomed Gerry, in his gruffly Scottish accent.

Dr Radford ambled over to his favourite stool and claimed his spot.

"What can I get you Bob?" said Gerry.

"A Guinness please?"

"I don't know why I even ask," said Gerry with his Golem smile out already, "so what have you been doing with yourself now?"

"Ah nothing, just on my way back from the shopping mall."

"That Heathenish cesspit," rumbled Gerry, ever the dramatic.

Dr Radford laughed through his nose between sips of his beer, "I know," he said, "but I was getting a card for my wife's birthday. I had the present, but in true fashion, I forgot the card again."

"Oh right, what did you get her then?"

"A spa weekend away."

"Jesus I didn't have you down for someone who liked cucumbers over his eyes," Gerry teased.

"Oh, it won't be me that goes," said Dr Radford whimsically, "she'll go with one of her friends."

Gerry finally finished wiping down the already clean top, "And how are the wife and kid keeping?"

"Yes, good thanks. Can you believe this nonsense?" irked Dr Radford, dodging questions about his daughter, pointing at the old television above them. *Doomsday passes again* read the subtitles.

"You're telling me pal, I had to listen to it on repeat for weeks on this channel. I wished it was true to put me out of my misery."

Dr Radford swallowed his drink hastily to scratch the itch on his mind, "It's funny you should say that," he pointed, "because I was almost thinking people seem to wish these worldwide disasters would happen. Are we that bored? Wait until people can't get their nails done at the mall, that'll be real anarchy."

"I don't know, I'm holding out for the zombie apocalypse myself. I fancy myself as a bit of a Rick Grimes, Walking Dead hero, d'you know what I mean?" said Gerry

"I won't lie Gerry, I pictured you more as the tubby one from Sean of the Dead, waiting for it all to blow over with a pint at the Winchester."

"Oh, would you look at that," curled Gerry's lip, "One-Sip-Bob piping up again hey," he joked.

"Anyway," Dr Radford continued preaching unperturbed, "we always need some existential threat, it's just a case of what next? China is our number one trading partner and we get scared they're planning World War Three with us."

"Ah but wait now Bob, do you really trust the Chinese? They cover up more than a Muslim woman robbing a bank."

"Well to be honest no," he said, "I'm just ranting, and probably as sick of the status quo as all the conspiracy theorists, just on the other side of the picket line. I just hope when the real disaster strikes we're united. I know too well from work how divided people are in this society, the young and old, rich and poor, black and white, the same old story people are tired of living."

"Amen Bob."

Sometimes Dr Radford's thoughts ran away with themselves.

"You know what, maybe people want the world to end so we can start over? No debt, no social class, no more stuck in a shitty job, no more expectations."

"Sounds alright to me," said Gerry, "people will still always want a beer."

"I tell you what though, at least if another worldwide crisis happens most will gain a bit of perspective, our parents and grandparents had World War Two for their lessons. But who knows I'm rambling."

"You know Bob, you intellectuals get your knickers in a twist debating every nuance and searching for something new to say, but I often find my answers in the simple life lessons handed down by my dear nan, for some people the grass is always greener on the other side, and life is what you make it, what more do you need to know? Forget all about career expectations and money, when you're lying on your deathbed you just want one more day in the sun with your wife and girlfriend."

"Cheers to that," conceded Dr Radford.

Their glasses hit the wooden top, and the hand ticked past *3*, *4*, and *5*. The evening bodies filled the room, and with their fluttering mouths time flew by. But Dr Radford's dark thoughts still held onto the butterfly, broken winged and beautiful, in his mind's eye, and in the bottom of each pint glass.

WHATEVER COMES NEXT

8th JULY

Two months had passed since Vincent's attack, and Leon was having zero success finding those responsible. He asked his contacts in the security business and Vincent's in the drug game, "I have no idea," he was told, "I can't help you," they said.

Either people were too scared to say anything, or these attackers were aliens. He even got his buddy Jack who worked at the gas station to show him the footage from that night. The camera had a good view out onto Olympic Boulevard, but all he saw was a grainy image of the van being driven by a white guy with dark hair. And that was hardly a lead of promise.

After a month, when Vincent's condition improved and he went home from the hospital, enthusiasm for revenge began to wane. In fact, Vincent was surprisingly upbeat. Leon thought it was because the loss of his leg had actually given Vincent an easy way out of crime, and a quick disability pay check. Apart from anything else, Vincent loved his new found attention.

"You wait till I get my robotic leg, I'm going to be Robo Thug."

He would tell anyone that would listen. Leon's worry also subsided with Vincent's growing esteem, but he knew better than to forget what happened that night. He slept with a gun under his bed, a Browning Hi Power semi-automatic. At times Leon questioned his own readiness for violence, but he needed to be prepared for whatever comes next. He had been here before, in the calm waters after the first wave. Crime was starting to rise again in this city. Maybe from apathy, maybe from drugs, maybe from poverty. They only thing the authorities could decide upon was to fix the figures. Leon knew it would just be a matter of time before he was caught up in another situation. Whether it was some new shit with Vincent or a problem from his time under the Los Muertos Cartel.

A year ago, going by the name Chris McLane in San Antonio Texas, he took a simple Personal Investigation job for a friend, on a low-level lawyer. The trouble began when he discovered the lawyer was depositing money for a rival gang of his supposed friend, Leroy. The next step was his first mistake. He agreed to show Leroy and a few of his pals the evidence in person. Before he could say anything, never mind reason with them, the gang in his vehicle jumped out and executed the lawyer by firing squad. Turns out the gang was part of a cartel, and that was it. He was in the game. The Los Muertos Cartel thought a kid like

Leon might talk, but Leroy vouched for his useful-
ness and they shipped him to La Cabellera, Mexico. He
quickly proved his worth as a courier and security for
the bosses, until a deadly shootout with another rival
gang at their base gave Leon the chance to jump ship.
He killed the last remaining men on both sides and
drove for days, tactically laying low for a while, before driving straight across the border to LA, only to
foolishly get involved in a car chase with police fifteen
minutes from home. When a police car passed these
days, sometimes his skin forgot to get Goosebumps,
but the weight never left him.

  A couple weeks after his date with Ellie, Leon started
working night time security for a local scrap yard
business. Vincent knew the owner of the place and
it was certainly shady, but it kept Leon occupied and
almost legitimate. His employment was kept off the
books, all cash in hand.

  "How much you looking to get paid?" asked the boss.

  "Your basic wage."

Leon didn't need the money, he just wanted to live
normally. Each night on the job he watched twilight
contour shapes and colours over the scrap yard. And
when the iridescent sky faded to night, he found solitude in its nothingness, ready for the sunrise to wake
his thoughts again. It was the easiest job he ever had.
The best part was his boss Walt sorting him out with
a classic car from the yard. A 1969 Pontiac Beaumont,
in lemon yellow. The rusty shell needed restoring, but
suddenly he had a hobby. And soon enough driving

to work under the moonlight his grip on the wheel relaxed. There was nothing quite like driving on an empty highway with a clear mind to make him feel like he was at peace.

He had also come to enjoy Ellie's company as a welcome distraction from himself and his problems. They saw each other at least three times a week, and despite his cold nature he managed to make her smile. They went to the cinemas for comedy movies, fancy restaurants for romantic dates, or sometimes by accident they just drove around for hours and spoke, she would always choose. And she would always interest him, even her irreverent idiosyncrasies.

"I wish they would make coffee lip balm, it would really save me time with both," she said getting dressed in the morning.

"That's a thing."

"Oh," she laughed, "trust you to know."

These stray thoughts of hers would rise without filter, sometimes with an undertone of unhappiness.

"I used to imagine one day I'd be living in Argentina," she announced supine to the sky, "with two kids: a boy and a girl. In a house on a hill that overlooked the ocean. Not even a big house, just one made of old wood. And I'd lay there with my husband watching my life go by with the sound of the ocean rocking me to sleep."

"That's a pretty picture," he said.

"Can we go one day?"

"Where?"

"To Argentina," Ellie mimicked the worst Hispanic accent ever, saved by her innocent smile.

"One day."

It was easy for them to forget their real circumstance, and pretend without noticing that everything was going to be okay. That he wasn't on the run, and she wasn't suicidal.

"I think I'm starting to fall for you," Ellie whispered one night when they were half asleep in bed.

"Okay let me know when you do," Leon made light of the situation. He was afraid of hurting her because as much as he tried to forget it, danger would return to his life someday. So he let his secrets pervade a space between them. Leon hoped one day soon she would grow strong enough not to need anyone, especially him, if he had to leave. But he was also scared that if her depression returned, she would stop everyone from helping.

Ellie recounted her childhood stories like flippant anecdotes.

"It was mundanely interesting at best," she said, "though don't get me wrong I had an uncomfortable beginning."

Her parents were never a real couple, just two teenagers brought together by a surprise pregnancy. Ellie's father was always a trucker, and eventually, his journeys grew longer and longer until he didn't come home. She never saw him again after her ninth birthday. Nonetheless, as a child, it never bothered Ellie, if you believed her. It was always Ellie and her mom against everything else.

She remembered being a happy kid, popular at school and forever outside playing. Football, My Little Pony, tiaras - she was involved. Then somewhere within her early teenage existence, she became uneasy with her own expectations. Football, My Little Pony and tiaras became silly games, and in their place was a void.

"It's puberty, deal with it," Ellie had been warned.

Other girls moved onto boys, makeup or alcohol, and she did try them, but sadness remained inside her. Until one day aged fifteen she read the novel *Sophie's World* by Jostein Gaarder, and she was engaged. Invigorated by a feeling of self-knowledge she searched for all the philosophers referenced in the book, pursuing her spirituality. Re-incarnation, pantheism and all the other isms - she strung pieces of ideas together, trying to find her own ideology. But there's only so long you can live inside your head, and before long she drifted back to wanting the validation of her peers, back to alcohol, boys and Instagram modelling as her new escape. Yet still the void remained. Ellie told Leon the first time she tried to kill herself was aged sixteen with sleeping pills.

Still hope made a fool of Leon, when each time he saw Ellie she seemed more natural in her words and body. Until the quiet moments, when she laid still and the world around her had stopped, Ellie became lost in herself again. She would stare into thoughts Leon did not know, and he would long for when she used to just blurt out her unhappiness. Ellie continued to

visit psychiatrists and received regular anti-depres-
sant medication, despite his objection.

"I still need help," she screamed.

Leon argued with her but each time less so, not wanting to push Ellie away. After all, he knew she was like
this when he first met her. Leon would chat to Dr Radford most times he visited the hospital, both for his
grandma and now with Ellie. Maybe he goes out of his
way to be nice because he feels sorry for me, thought
Leon. Either way, they seemed to be on the same side,
and he used the opportunity to try and convince the
Dr - with subtle comments and implied notions - that
Ellie did not belong in the hospital on medication.
"You know I can't discuss other patients with you
buddy," said Dr Radford, or "Robert," as he insisted
on being called. Leon still thought he was making a
difference.

Though he could not stop the great changes to his
grandma. Each passing week eroded another chip
from her memory, and what remained was abstract.
Leon visited her often, and increasingly her thoughts
became more fragmented, and her actions erratic.
She remembered him mostly, but sometimes only by
name.

"Where is the other Leon?" she would ask.

"I am Leon."

"No, no not you, my Leon."

Maybe she only remembered a younger version of
him. She became even skinnier than she already was,
her limbs sticking out of her knitwear like protruding

bones. Eating food was an occasional habit she would suffer only when he promised cakes or something else sweet. She became withdrawn and afraid, unable to know her environment or the people around her she had a constant desire to leave. They would move from one room to the next on her insistence, and she would shout, "You can't keep me here," when the nurses shut the entrance door.

She did escape once and somehow managed to make it ten miles away on public transport, before being found asking for help by a stranger. Despite these episodes, there were good times, made of simple conversations which kept her identity alive.

"I'm really glad you are here today, Leon," she would say squeezing his hand.

These times made Leon glad he returned home, yet life had become surreal. Every passing billboard or TV advert appeared satirical despite its intentions, and daily problems were melodramas when viewed in greater scope. He welcomed bad days with his Nan with the same attitude he had for the happy days spent with Ellie, with patient reservation. He knew that change would always come, and this lullaby would end. He could not allow himself to be trapped into believing otherwise, for better or worse. He could only be ready.

BAPTISM

He beat his head against the roof of the trunk and kept hitting it, long after the plastic had burned a laceration on his forehead.

The banging was hopelessly lost within the thrashing of the motor, and he resigned himself to his fate. In the darkness he rest his head on the floor, letting his burned skin stick to the carpet, with the abyss gazing back at him.

Finally the car slowed and they came to an abrupt halt, bouncing his head on the ceiling. The chime of the opening trunk caused his hair to stand on end. A heavy shadow cast over him. By his collar the shadow tossed him face first into the ground outside, and from his ankles he was dragged into the blinding beams of the car's headlights, sneezing out mud as he went, crying for his children. Between the white lights the figure of Donnie leered at his tears, stretching a rubber glove over his hand and letting it snap back comically.

"Surprise," yelled Donnie like a chat show host.

He released a muffled scream through the rag in his mouth, reduced to an animal bowling around in the dirt, fighting for his last breaths in the world, but unable to escape the ties to his hands and feet. Below still trees uncaring to his despair, alone in the silent woodland, he looked out at a tranquil lake, castaway from help, but for some desperate reason looking to roll towards the water.

Donnie stuck a boot on his chest to keep him from moving.

"Hey," said Donnie all friendly, "look at me, I said look at me," Donnie pressed his boot down harder, "that's better."

He beheld Donnie with haunted eyes and every muscle shaking his loose jowls, close to exorcism.

"I liked your speech the other day Josh," said Donnie, "Josh Moogana? Ogbanna? Anyway, your speeches, always so profound, so emotional, always so weak and afraid. I thought the blacks were empowered. You know, fighting the powers that be? Never mind."

"By the way, I'm glad you all bought my performance," his theatrical drawl continued, "it's a new character I'm bedding in. One close to my heart," he said holding his chest and lunging his face close to Josh's.

"You know, I was afraid once. As a kid, I was frightened of bullies. I was scared of my family too, and I was too weak to fight back. In the end, I became afraid of everything, even living. I would wake up and pass through the day like walking in a dream," Donnie snapped his fingers like a magician, "so, one day when I was fourteen I hung myself from the balcony of our fifth floor apartment, clinging onto the ledge with my fingertips. I looked down at the concrete ground and I could feel it. The cold plates crushing my bones. But, I strained every muscle in my fingers and reached up and grabbed the rail. I pulled myself up, and I stood on the ledge looking down at the concrete again, and you know what? I was no longer afraid."

Josh tried to writhe away from Donnie's grasp in vain.

"Then I killed a few family pets and blah blah, you can guess how the rest of the story goes because you're right here," Donnie fake smiled, pupils dilated, visualising violence.

Across the lake, three more shadows stood guard around the edges of the water, a mile around in a triangle formation. Donnie rose his fist up straight in a frozen salute, and the shadows mimicked him. Josh shovelled his head into the mud as hard as he could, his muffled screams battling louder and louder, but he could not stop Donnie pulling him into the lake. Donnie lay him on the surface of the water and took the rag out of his mouth.

"Help me," Josh cried.

"I am," said Donnie, diving Josh's head under the water.

"This is your baptism."

With only small ripples disturbing the lake's sleep, Donnie held him there until his body stopped wriggling.

YOUR NORMAL
LIFE

1st AUGUST

Max pondered the picture of missing Heather Dodd. Eye to eye, runaway to runaway, all the way into the pixels. Unfortunately in her job, the faces of victims could sometimes be lost in the crowd. But she studied Heather's face down to the freckles. Determined to see, hear and feel her cries for help, because if she could reunite Heather with her family, it would be worth all the square eyes from laptop screens and stupid arguments at home. She would be able to feel a purpose.

"Captain says Chief wants to see you two."

Max swivelled around in her office chair, yelling, "Why?" with cake in her mouth.

Joe Schembri didn't elaborate, so she just watched his swaying ass walk away.

Denzel hit Max's arm, "Stop checking him out

woman."

Max kept watching, almost sliding off her seat.

"Come on now, drop the cake too it could be serious," Denzel said rising to his feet, "let's see what we're in for."

Max marched in line behind him, and said, "Why do you have to be so tall? I feel like I'm being marched to the principal's office."

"If it's about reading the rights to the passed-out wino last week let me do the talking."

It was a tawdry summer night, humid as hell at 8PM, after a long day safeguarding vulnerable adults. Including sitting with a victim of domestic violence for three hours in her house while the team found the husband. They could have left earlier but Denzel insisted they wait. It was just too bad the paperwork couldn't wait tonight too. With Denzel's guidance, after a nervy start, Max was settling into being a detective nicely, or at least so she thought.

Denzel knocked twice to be polite and once for good luck on Chief's door.

"Come in."

They stood to attention, as the Chief browsed her papers nonchalantly. The dry air conditioning made Max cough nervously.

"Have a seat please," they were told.

They sat down in the two empty chairs waiting for them, and Max adjusted her increasingly uncomfortable tie.

"So," Chief said sternly, "I've got bad news, Heather

Dodd was murdered."

Max pulled her tie loose, feeling wheezy, "How?" escaped from her mouth.

"Dissolved in concentrated hydrochloric acid."

"Jesus," muttered Denzel in shock.

Not a muscle in Chief's face flinched at the news - she could not allow it.

"I know you will both be disappointed not to find Heather, but rest assured we will find the killer. We're going to widen the team, a forensics report will be sent to you and I'm going to be heavily involved in this case going forward."

"Thank you, Ma'am," said Denzel.

"Where did they find her?" asked Max disbelieving.

"A barrel was placed outside our United States District Court, seeping blood and had a letter stuck on the outside, which read:

Dear leaders of the swamp. Abort underage pregnancies, deport all illegal immigrants and increase the top rate income tax back to 91%. Or I will keep killing those whom you fail to fix.

Apparently, a man was simply walking his dog and the animal started going crazy at the barrel, enough to get the owner spooked enough to call the station. We believe the body to be Heather's because the killer left her Christian Confirmation bracelet undissolved in the mess, with inscriptions her parents could identify."

"Heather was pregnant, right? So that's why she was targeted?" asked Denzel.

"That is a connection we should consider."

"So we have a potential serial killer on our hands here? And we also have to try and protect all illegal immigrants and the rich?" Max's incredulity grew and her tone fell inappropriately.

"I also want you to ask a different question," Chief replied still phlegmatic, "where did the killer get this acid from? To choose that method – if we're looking at a serial killer – he or she might have a lot of it. Could it have been stolen or maybe our killer just bought it from the thief?"

Denzel nodded at all the right times, trying to hide his disappointment but sucking a lemon.

"It's a tenuous lead I know," continued Chief, "but we haven't got a lot else right now. Handwriting experts are taking a look at the note, but as you know, this can be unreliable. We will wait to see if forensics can shed any further light, or maybe our IT guys pin-down suspected buyers online, but in the meantime let's investigate those with access to such chemicals in the local area, especially our current suspects."

"Maybe they're a factory worker," Denzel jumped to the nearest conclusions with her.

"Aren't nearly all factories here closed these days?" quipped Max.

Awkward silence answered her first, before Denzel said, "Some, so it makes the search even easier for us."

"I'm sorry Chief, I just, I just really hoped we had

more evidence," Max crumbled, "it's one of those cases where I actually worry for Alicia's safety out there right now. You don't always realise killers like this are there in your neighbourhood."

"Relax," whispered Denzel.

"It's fine Denzel, it's fine," Chief calmed them both.

She reached over her desk and spun around a photo frame.

"Who is that?"

"That Max is me at a Meatloaf concert in 1994. See me hugging Meatloaf in the sweaty t-shirt? Yeah, you can tell by his where-the-fuck-is-security face he didn't like that, but I didn't care. You know sometimes, I look at it and think it's silly to have this picture here when I'm dealing with serious cases about life and death. But then again, when I get to go home as a bat out of hell, how big a deal is life and death anyway. Do you know what I mean?"

Max didn't know what Chief meant, however, she managed to compose herself, saying, "I think so."

"I'm surprised, because there's many things about our jobs which don't make sense, but trust me, when it's over, you will be able to return to your normal life at home, except you will actually enjoy it. We all appreciate the fine work you two are doing, now is the time to keep pushing."

"Thank you – thank you Ma'am," the Detectives fought to say it first.

"Where are we with the current suspects for the case?"

"They all have a credible alibi, except one man who remains unaccounted for from the CCTV that night," Denzel answered, "it seems he knew when to keep his head down in the club, but we do know he was wearing a distinctive leather jacket, is around 6'4" and has a detailed tribal tattoo crawling up from his neck. Additional CCTV from around the area has also so far been inconclusive in identifying his face."

"Interesting, please continue to pursue this individual and consolidate the information we have. Now that we're looking at a murder case, we may be putting this description to the public soon. Thank you," Chief said returning to read her papers.

"We're on it Chief."

After the detectives left, Chief chucked the photo frame in the draw of her desk, taking out a bottle of pills in exchange. For good measure, she threw three pills down her throat without swallowing any water, and in the PC monitor fixed her fringe with a wavering hand.

Outside, Denzel stopped dead in his tracks.

"What is it?" said Max.

"We're not going back to our desks – this way."

SHARDS OF WHITE FIRE

4th AUGUST

The storm raged into the night, blanketing the city with biblical rain and lightning shards spreading like white fire, dancing behind the window. Knock, knock, said thunder.

"Leon," called his Nan across the garden, on a summer's day in years passed.

"Leon," she screamed from the window's reflection, with her face writhing in pain.

He turned around and could only watch the nurses pin her down.

"Help me?" she pleaded with him.

It took three nurses to wrestle her arm out straight, while a doctor tried to find a lasting vein on her needle-ravaged arm. She clenched her jaw and snarled with hatred, belching shrieks of agony. Leon took his grandma's hand in his, and like a vice she clenched his fingers.

"Why did you let them do this to me?" her eyes begged him, drowning in tears.

"They're helping you," said Leon.

"No they're hurting me."

"It's okay."

A doctor managed to inject the sedatives and she screamed until her voice broke, collapsing like her soul had been torn out.

"All done now," said a young Thai nurse, rubbing her eyebrows off with forearm sweat, and speaking too soon. A fist swung from his grandma and reverberated off the nurses' chubby arm.

"Don't you ever do that again," his Nan yelled.

The tired nurse kissed her lips with disdain, but left it there, walking away.

Leon's grandma had a UTI infection and was carried into hospital last night with a fever. The infection and hospital drugs had taken their toll, causing delirium.

"Help me please, help me?" she called through the night, trapped in a loop within her semi-conscious state. For the last three hours she had repeated the same verse, with Leon reciting the promise, "I will."

"Oh, you will? Oh, thank you nurse thank you," she said almost smiling, but the comfort soon slipped away like a forgotten dream, and the cry returned, "help me please, help me."

She had only come to recognise Leon again when she saw his reflection in the glass, like the ghost he had now become.

Leon was not one to feel pain sharply. He had been carved into a stoic figure, embalmed by the things he had done, things he had seen, but he was a walking contradiction. He had been raised by his grandma from the age of eight after his parents were killed in a skiing accident. The cliffs were incorrectly signed apparently, he never asked to hear the story twice. He didn't remember crying, but he was promised he did. It didn't matter - pity was not a luxury he could afford on the lowly streets of the city.

He grew up on the boulevards lined with graffiti, running in filth and breathing in the dust swept down from the other side of town. The kids weren't taught to feel sorry for themselves here, so they didn't care much about being left behind anyway. His grandma was a victim of both worlds. She had strived with hard working principles from poverty to make it, only to still be left with nothing and no one, in expensive care homes and hospitals, dirtying clean sheets.

As he watched her now, Leon was a boy again, unravelled from the barriers he had built. He wasn't born uncaring, the world was, except of course, his Nan's love.

"Are you going to stay with her?" asked the returning Thai nurse, with her crooked self-aware smile pleading with him.

"Yes, a little longer," he said, taking his turn to leave the room for some respite.

Into the corridor, the bacteria filled air followed him and festered in his mind too. Leon slouched against the wall to rest his eyes when his phone vibrated in his pants.

Phone me – Vincent, the text read.

Leon chucked the phone back in his pocket, only for the phone to vibrate again minutes later.

(323) 324-4158 calling

Leon didn't recognise the number, so he answered the phone but waited for them to speak.

"Hello, Leon? It's Robert," spoke Dr Radford, "you there?"

"Yes."

"Hi, I just wanted to let you know, I'm sorry to hear about your grandma. The care home called through this morning. I hope she has a speedy recovery and I look forward to catching up with her and yourself soon. Also, I just want to let you know," stammered the Dr, "well maybe I shouldn't be telling you this, or maybe you already know, but Ellie tried to kill herself last week."

Leon did not know.

"It's important we all keep an eye on her and look out for her right now. And if you need to talk about anything, just let me know... You still there?"

"Yeah I'm here. Thank you, Bob, for calling, I appreciate it."

"No problem. If you want to talk, you know where my office is."

"Sure. Thanks, take care," said Leon.

"Okay now. Bye, buh-bye, bye."

Leon hung up the phone and closed his eyes again,

falling through the hole before him, and arising with a fury, taking his iPhone in his grasp and watching it smash apart on the ground. With each rising breath, he stamped on the phone, grinding his teeth and panting through his nose, until the phone became jigsaw pieces.

The young nurse stuck her head out of the doorway with scared eyes running wide, not recognising the calm and collected man she saw before.

"I will be back soon," Leon told her.

Leon composed himself to walk evenly down the corridors and out of the hospital, stopping beneath the pelting rain. He returned to the hole in his mind and let the rain fill it. He could feel the water creeping up to his neck, ready to drown him, and he let it. Until thunder awoke him, and he watched the lightning strike the buildings above him again, waiting to see if one would strike him, but they did not.

Leon strolled across the road to the parking lot, got in his Pontiac and switched on the ignition loudly to match the thunder. The wheels skid on his washed-out thoughts and he drove on, listening to sports commentary coming from the radio:

> *"A UFC Bantamweight Championship rematch between current two-time champion T.J. Dillashaw and former champion Cody Garbrandt will headline UFC 227 tonight…"*

His subconscious strained to rise Dr Radford's phone

call to his thoughts, but Leon let the sound of rain be a background interference, and the window wipers beat to his rising tension. Stop. He slammed his foot on the breaks – almost crashing into the stationary van ahead. The possibility of Ellie dying was an after-thought he had buried long ago, after silently assum-ing their relationship had changed her outlook on life.

Leon drove into the basement parking lot of his apartment and stopped in his usual space by the cor-ner. In a haze he pressed *level 8* in the elevator, and leant on the rail, gazing up at the white light, and down at the mirror in front of him. It was a fucking mistake coming back, he thought.

From mousey hair his palm crept down his face, from his cheekbones to his chin, stretching tired skin. The spotlights formed shadows in the shape of his skull, and death stared back at him briefly, as the lift stopped at *level 3*, and the doors slid open to a woman stood holding hands with a little boy.

"Come on now Lucian," she said up-talking in south-ern Californian, "over here."

The child shuffled between her legs, standing oppos-ite Leon against the mirror. The mother was about five-nothing with dark braids down to her butt, watching him wearily with smooth black skin on a round face flecked with dimples, wide nostrils, small dashes for eyebrows and puffed lips saying, "Every-thing alright?"

Leon realised he must have been staring and said, "Yes sorry, I was daydreaming."

"Oh, not to worry," she politely laughed, with glossy teeth showing.

"You didn't get caught in the rain then?"

"Oh no," she said, "We haven't been out, I was just taking my son to see his grandparents, they live on the third floor."

The little boy clung onto her leg like a koala and looked just like her, with doe-eyes observing Leon.

"Yeah I think I've seen them," remembered Leon, "they grow tomatoes on their balcony?"

"Yes, yes that's them," she chuckled, "that's my crazy parents. They never leave that balcony. So, you live here then?"

"Yeah eighth floor."

"Ah okay, we live on the seventh. You know I'm surprised we haven't seen you around here before, are you new?" she said with almond eyes still investigating him.

"I was just gone for a while."

"Oh okay, you staying for long this time?" she asked.

"Mom where's Dad?" squeaked the boy.

"He's at work," Mom said rubbing his afro.

"I'm thinking about it," Leon answered.

The lift's buzzer dinged at the display of *level 7* and the silver doors glided open.

"Good to meet you," she said seeming genuine, "I'm Linda by the way."

"Have a good evening."

"Goodbye," said the boy as they left, and the mother beamed proud of him, waiving bye at Leon too. Lucky family, he thought, catching himself smiling in the mirror. The metal doors slid shut on that moment and opened at *level 8*, leaving Leon to stand outside his apartment, staring at the black door in sombre silence.

Come on, he said to himself, and opened the door, noticing Ellie's keys hanging up. Like it was a normal Saturday, Leon grabbed a Budweiser from the fridge and watched TV in the neatly tidied living room. Ellie had been busy.

"*Thiago Santos wins by unanimous decision,*" sounded the television, as UFC played out.

In her Christmas PJ's, Ellie skipped into the room and jumped up beside him on the sofa.

"What you watching?" she put on a kids voice.

"UFC, it was left on the sports channel."

"Of course, the sports channel," she joked.

He took a long sip of his beer.

"Who is playing?" asked Ellie.

"Well, this is the undercard to Dillashaw vs. Garbrandt, two bantamweights in a rematch for the title after Dillashaw won by KO last time."

"Oh cool," Ellie feigned interest, glancing at the television only between takes of Leon's face, and humming an imaginary song for attention. Leon ignored her, taking another swig of his beer.

"Everything okay?" said Ellie confused.

"Yeah, how was your meeting today?"

"Yeah-no it was good," she fumbled, before confidently saying, "I had another one-to-one with Dr Radford, to see how the meds were working, and then we had a little group thing and it went okay, they're all happy with me."

"So, you're feeling better now, right?"

"I guess so," she shrugged with melancholy.

"We need to be honest with each other," pleaded Leon, unmoved from his stare at the television.

"What?" Ellie was taken aback.

"Dr Radford phoned."

"What?" she asked again, red-faced and guilty-eyed but still trying to smile like normal.

Leon finally turned to face her. Still startled, her mouth could only grasp empty words.

"Dr Radford called and said you tried to take your life last week?" his tone softened.

"You went behind my back?" Ellie leapt to her defence and feet, "You went behind my back and spoke to my Doctor? What the fuck?"

"That's what you have to say?" Leon asked disappointed.

"I don't know what you want me to say," she refused to engage.

"Just tell me why? Please?"

"It's being blown out of proportion, okay, it was the anniversary of my mother's death and I took more medication than usual because I was feeling pretty shit. But it was a mistake, as you can see, I'm fine and it's not going to happen again. I can't believe you spoke to my Doctor."

After being caught off guard by Leon knowing the

truth, Ellie had composed herself enough to try and deflect shame onto him. Their masks were on and the gloves off, as they acted out roles detached from their true feelings for each other.

"You're promising it won't happen again?" he said, trying not to sound sarcastic.

"Listen this is unfair, you know this is unfair," she began to cry, "my problems are my problems and I don't need you putting pressure on me like this. You can't expect me to change for you, I am not a damsel in distress, and you are not the strong man who fixes me."

Any pretence Leon had fell with her tears, as he said, "I'm so sorry Ellie. I did hope I was making you happy, but I never saw you as broken."

"That's the problem," she shouted.

"I can't do this anymore, I'm going," she barely whispered.

Leon knew he should have said something else or tried to stop her, but he only watched her leave. The door slammed shut on the future he imagined, the happy home, the carefree holidays, the other side of life. I should never have tried, he thought. The storm was only being polite by knocking. He took another swig of his beer and got back to watching the fights, trying not to look at the splashed tear drops beside him.

THE ROCKING CHAIR

The rocking chair creaked over Donnie's maniacal laughter. Between flashes of the television, out of darkness. In the reel of pictures he grinned with bleeding gums and canine teeth, squinting bloodshot eyes, high as hell.

"Don't you love this shit?" he yelled spitting chips, "Hey Henry?"

"Fuck yeah," gabbled Henry.

Henry was sprawled on the bedroom floor, giving Donnie's red eye good competition. Through the curtains of greasy ginger hair he was transfixed on the ceiling, seeing magic dragons out of nothing. Bloody too was his nose, flattened sideways like an old boxer. Not that he was bothered, dribbling from his flaking lips like a happy toddler, onto milky skin.

> "Oh no he's fallen at the last hurdle, Ninja Warrior can be so cruel, only the greatest survive."

Donnie swivelled his head around, and said amused, "You're cracked out again, aren't you Henry?"

Henry ensured there was no doubt by wetting himself.

"You're missing out."

The echo of a slamming door dispersed through the building, shaking dust off the decrepit walls and pricking Donnie's ears. Footsteps approached the room, making clunking sounds on floorboards. Through the swinging door entered two men - one ducking his head under the frame, the other taking two steps just to make it inside. Donnie relaxed at his family's return and put the .357 revolver back on the table.

The big man wore a skinhead with faded tribal tattoos for hair, crawling from his neck over his shiny dome and encircling his right eye. A gold crucifix earring hung from his left ear, the other one was half chewed off. With his flat snout twitching and his cheeks bulging, he looked like a hateful bulldog.

Stood beside him, a foot down, was an uneven creature with buck teeth giving him a rat's face, and large unblinking pupils waiting for Donnie's approval. He scratched a nest on his head and twitched fuzzy eyebrows like something was the matter.

Both wore shapeless jackets, the big man in leather and the other a raincoat, in tattered jeans which could have been cut from one thread. Most importantly for the family, they were both white as Aryans.

"And where have you been Franco?" asked Donnie

through the back of his head.

"Just at a bar," drawled Franco, frozen in his boots and glancing at a dribbling Henry for support.

Donnie sauntered towards them with the revolver in hand, and surveyed their bodies from head-to-toe, noticing scratch marks on Franco's neck.

"Then why, is there mud on your shoes?" crooned Donnie.

The pair looked down at their filthy boots, and Donnie seized the chance – pistol whipping Franco to the floor, and bouncing his thick skull off the boards. Before the ground stopped shaking Donnie sprung a six inch blade from his overalls, and held its sharp edge against the throat of the little man still standing.

"You've been acting without my permission again haven't you?" Donnie asked with sarcastic enthusiasm.

"We –

"Did you kill someone?"

"No," Nichols cried, kneeling down with his hands up in surrender, and joining his partner on the floor.

Donnie held the knife up like a butcher mid swing, waiting for them to speak, eerily tranquil.

"We picked her up from a fancy bar," murmured Franco.

"You stupid fucks," screamed Donnie, hurling the knife at the wall behind them.

"No it's okay she fits the plan," said Franco, "right, Nichols?"

"You've got a lot to say Sasquatch," Donnie interjected.

Nichols stood up defiantly, all 5'4" of him, and said, "It's true Don, we caught her celebrating her banking bonus or something," he yapped wiping his coke nose.

Hesitantly Franco copied his partner's courage, slowly rising to his feet, "And she was alone, her friend was sick and had gone home, no witnesses," he said.

Donnie's rage slipped to wonder, "And she told you ugly fucks all of this? You hardly look like Santa's fucking helpers, or maybe you do you little shit," he pointed at Nichols, "how do you two even get into an expensive bar, huh?"

"We met her in the pizzeria on the same street, no cameras, and we brought her straight here," said Nichols.

"Where is she?" Donnie licked his lips and scattered his eyes between them.

Franco and Nichols led Donnie out of the room and through the hall of the dilapidated building. Their feet crunched rubble in the dust filled warehouse, and they stepped into a murky garage. A red and rusty third generation Ford Ranger sat beneath a floodlight, and a muffled squeal rang like tinnitus in the air.

"You brought her here, to our hideout, not even fucking dead?" Donnie laughed.

"We thought you would want to handle it," said Nichols with sorry eyes.

"Oh I will, but you two are going to clean up."

The trunk of the car rose with desperate squeals escaping only so far as Donnie.

"We soundproofed the room, baby," Donnie said open armed towards the foam walls.

Curled up like a foetus the middle-aged woman lay facing away from him. Donnie dragged her out stiletto first, ripping her floral dress. With a screech she hit the ground and curled up again. Donnie stepped over the woman's body for attention, kneeling down face-to-face. As they touched noses she reeled from him, starting to hyperventilate. Her fiery hazel eyes tried to burn Donnie, but instead he gently ran his fingers through her auburn hair, admiring soft features and freckles.

"Reminds me of my mom," said Donnie warmly, "good job boys."

The woman gurned her jaw to try and break free from the gaffer tape. The family didn't even try to stop her. Over the shoulders of Donnie, Nichols and Franco only ogled the woman, watching her feeble attempts to escape as part of the show.

"I think she wants to speak," said Donnie, ripping off the tape – but she stopped making a sound. Afraid, she buried her face in the dust away from them.

"Maybe not," quipped Donnie, "pass me the gloves."

Franco handed him lab safety gloves and Donnie snapped them back on his hands. From the dirt he raised and held the woman's chin in his palm, his other hand caressing the cold blade on her cheek. The woman's fiery eyes extinguished and her pupils ran from the knife, shutting left and right.

"So afraid," spoke Donnie solemnly, "don't worry, it's not your fault, and you're not the only one. I killed some suicidal people for practice, because who is going to notice? I've purged America of immigrants, you're welcome. And I've murdered rich people like you because the revolution is coming. It's just natural selection, really."

He raised the woman's face before his own, "Open your eyes."

In a single and graceful motion, Donnie cut the blade along her cheek. Like red tears the blood tricked down, yet the woman had stopped weeping, becoming bewildered in Donnie's gaze.

"Good, good, you should not fear such pain. The fear consumes you," he said, "nature's little control you see. The only way to die free is to embrace your pain. And you will, die today."

Donnie's thumb wiped her blood and old tears together.

"Take some solace in the feeling before you do, it is the only thing which binds us to life. And, you should know, if you scream you will only make it more fun for them."

"No," she wailed.

"Shhh," whispered Donnie, "I see you're wearing a cross."

On the tip of his finger he balanced the gold necklace, "Surely you are prepared for this then, no? Remember, the sky will roll back like a curtain and a pale horse will carry your body, as the rivers of time carry you through layers of memories. And then you will see it. The Tree of Life. And your mothers, fathers, sisters and brothers will all meet you, including those you did not know. For we were never really separate at all. But different masks on the same face, which when seen through the eyes of the creator, shows only a reflection."

"Please," she trembled.

"Or maybe there will be only darkness. After all, your god left you here, right?"

Donnie dropped her head back into the muck and put his serious voice on, "Dismember and dissolve her. You fucked up bringing her here, there can be no trace this time."

"No please God," she cried, as they dragged her to her end.

CHASING SHADOWS

15ᵗʰ AUGUST

High above the convoy of traffic, Max watched the passing plane blink red much calmer than their chirping police siren. Boxed into the riot van they raided a house in Downtown for illegal weapons and found crates full of firearms without serial numbers or somebody home. They were having little luck finding their suspects on a few cases, and on the way back to the station Max let it bother her.

"A damn grenade launcher, can you believe it?" asked a cheery Denzel.

"Mmhmm," replied Max, still fixed on the sky.

"What's up?"

"Maybe we should have talked to more neighbours," she said agitated.

"Oh yeah? Because ten wasn't enough?" Denzel asked sarcastically, "We found enough weapons in his property to put him away for years, it went okay."

"I think the guy next door knew more. Living there for four years and with a low fence he never saw him burying guns in the yard?"

"Jeez, there were neighbours all round he was just the only black one, do you profile me too?" Denzel joked.

"Because you're black?"

"Yeah?"

"Yeah-no being a raging feminist I prioritise that over my racism, and keep you in the male chauvinist category instead."

While Max's words were light-hearted, Denzel could easily tell something was weighing on her.

"You know I was only playing," he measured his response, "sometimes you can get too caught up in these cases, I promise you, there's always a new one."

"Yeah but we need to close more cases, and I'm just annoyed at myself, not you," Max apologised.

"Hold that thought," he said, as an incoming face-time call from Chief popped up on his mobile phone. For fuck sake, thought Max.

"Good afternoon Ma'am," answered Denzel.

Chiefs thumb-face filled the screen, and said, "Listen, I believe we have found our lead suspect in the Heather Dodd murder."

"Really?" they said.

"Yes let me finish. After the press was informed the case had changed to murder, an eye witness from the club that night has come into the station. She has given a detailed description which matches not only the missing suspect in the CCTV, but has positively identified one person from a photo-line up: Franco Egan. He has previous convictions of rape and battery, and has been wanted for the last three years on the charges of first degree murder of a police officer. I will be emailing you an updated case-file after this call and we can talk more in person."

"Great news Chief," said Max elated, "what's our next move?"

"The operation is already moving at speed. With the story in the press we have had several calls reporting sightings of our suspect's description, from Inglewood to Arizona. But, we have had repeated calls of sightings in East LA, and we're focusing our CCTV efforts here using Ai to try and identify Franco's face."

"Fantastic," said Denzel.

"Be ready for a call to move at speed should the CCTV review prove successful. We now have a serial killer to catch. I will also let you interview the eye witness yourself should you have any further questions. Bye for now."

The call ended before Max could decide which question to ask first. Away from her work computer - and unable to wait until the case-file was emailed – she googled *Franco Egan murder.* An old report of her fellow police officer being murdered came top of the rankings, and the case became even more personal. She stared into Franco's hooded eyes missing catch light, and thought, this is it.

Wild lights danced in the dark, red, blue and
white

As stars fell like dandelions in spring

His mad dreams fought with waking life tonight

Time's hand stroked his pale skin, cold, wise
and light

As blood fell from he who would be crowned
king

Wild lights danced in the dark, red, blue and
white

Four notes. Sixteen beats. The loud and beeping ring-tone awoke Leon. He reached across to his bedside table and grabbed the flashing light. *Vincent* read the caller ID on his new iPhone.

"Have you lost your second leg or can I go back to sleep?" answered Leon groggy.

"Ha... Ha. It is so too soon for that joke bro. So much so, that if I could find my right leg, my first action would be to beat you over the head with it. And it's only 1AM. What the hell? Get a nightlife."

"What do you want Vincent?"

"Listen now, this is important. I want you to get an Uber or train to 4801 Mesquit Street. I'm sat in a black

Ford Quest."

"No."

"This is important trust me man," Vincent moaned, "too important to explain over cell, you know what I mean?" he stretched his words for emphasis, "I will tell you everything when you are here."

Feeling sorry for Vincent, Leon breathed heavily over the phone to say yes.

"Yes brother," Vincent cheered, "thank you for this. You won't regret it."

"It will take me around twenty minutes."

"Thank you, thank you, I know bro. I will be waiting."

"If this isn't important-

"It is don't worry," Vincent jumped in.

"Okay see you then," Leon hung up.

In the silent night Leon absorbed some brief peace, closing his eyes for another moment. We go again, he whispered and sprung to life, switching on the bed-side lamp and walking over to his wardrobe. Probably a night for black, he thought, grabbing a sweatshirt and jogging bottoms. And maybe a disguise too, just in case.

From under the bed, Leon picked up a hyper realistic silicone mask of an East Asian man and his Browning Hi Power semi-automatic. In the silver of the gun he watched the warped reflection of his face and felt an uncanny feeling. He would not be making the same mistakes tonight, he thought, putting the mask and gun back and taking a Dallas Cowboys cap instead.

When Leon walked the streets the sirens played their

favourite emergency symphony, but the vibe in the air was calm. Everyone was used to the backing track. Hot and half naked couples and groups walked past Leon in their usual night life roles, the women cat walked and the guys watched Leon pass like protective dogs. People were civilised until you got closer to the clubs. That's why Leon stayed in and out of trouble watching *Breaking Bad* on repeat.

The train was filled with the same herd behaviour and more residents of the night - the drug addicts this time around. Leon sat with his cap low, being prodded in the arm by a wrinkly finger.

"Do you have any change for me boy?" three jagged teeth gabbled.

Behind eyes half cut, the old craggy man begged with sweat crawling from his pink bald head onto Leon's new Nike sneakers.

"No, sorry."

"Don't lie to me boy," the crackhead jabbed his long nail into Leon's shoulder.

Leon looked up from under his cap unhurried and into the man's cloudy eyes. With deliberate intent, he said, "If you touch me again, you will swallow the three teeth you have left."

The man staggered back, slipping on sick and flailing in his tracksuit.

"There's no need for that now," the old man whimpered, "I'm only an old man looking for help."

"I hope you find it. Have a good night."

The old beggar journeyed down the train tripping on

his own two feet, pleading, "Just trying to get money for a cab home."

Leon felt the watch of the passenger opposite.

"Were you really going to hit him?" spoke a well-worn silver voice.

"Of course not."

He stepped off the train at Metro Division 20, a few blocks away from Vincent and funnelled out of the streams of people. With each turn and new road his surroundings became more industrial, and the body count dwindled. Until it was only him, making lone echoes with his feet. Large spherical shapes rose above the moonlit skyline, making grey dreary factories look like art amongst the stars. Why am I here again? Leon remembered to ask.

He saw Vincent's car parked on the side of the road. Leon could tell for certain by the hanging pink dice, and the slug eyebrows looking at him from the rear-view mirror. Leon craned his neck around, looking for any other persons. The street was empty, so he quietly got into the passenger seat.

"My man you made it," Vincent greeted him.

Vincent looked like shit. He had eyes like a zombie and was a sickly yellow.

"Though we really should consult before we get dressed in the future," said Vincent, displaying his own black hoodie and bottoms.

"You look like shit, have you been smoking again?"

"Hell no," he protested.

"Then you're just about out of excuses as to why you

brought me here."

"Shhh man, have a look," said Vincent pointing ahead in the street.

Seventy metres behind the windshield stood metal railings ten feet tall that barricaded a wasteland of tarmac, scrap cars and tipped over bins. Oddly placed, the bars protected a tattered brick structure speckled with dirt and a yellow crane gantry which straddled the complex.

"What is this?"

"Used to be a warehouse for toys I've been told," said Vincent, "but we're not here to talk about your teddy bears."

Leon eye-balled him.

"All right, all right, all right," Vincent copied his favourite actor, "so I was watching the news and I see the police are searching for the killer of this school girl, seventeen and pregnant– big Middle America white tragedy. Think her surname is Dodd. An eye witness says the girl was last seen talking to a big guy with tattoos on his face at the Opium club. And then his face pops up," Vincent slapped the wheel…

"And it's the same motherfucker who was stomping on my face. Called Franco Egan. Full of the same tribal markings around his eyes, bald as fuck Neo-Nazi looking prick. Then I remember him laughing, with gums for days and crossed teeth. It was all too fucking vivid again, man. And the news say there's been sightings in East LA. Walking among us. How can I live like that? I won't. I fucking won't," Vincent grasped Leon furiously by his sleeve before realising he needed to relax, "so, I remember the direction that gang drove off in to narrow down my search, I'm driving for all day when I start thinking again about how this Franco knew where to rob our drugs? So I give the boss of distribution a call."

"The boss of your cocaine distribution?"

"Yeah and I send him the picture of this guy, and ask the boss if he recognises Franco? Maybe it was an inside job. He says yeah, Franco done some enforcing for me, and like you, I've seen him on the news wanted for murder, but don't worry, a birdy tells me the police have found him and are going to raid his hideout at 3AM. The boss doesn't even know Franco helped steal our drugs, he just doesn't want any blowback. So I ask him for the location, say I want to avoid the area and he tells me 4801 Mesquit Street."

"What the fuck Vincent? This is not avoiding the area," Leon struggled to suppress screaming.

"Because, I told you, I'm going to be the one to get revenge."

"Are there any police around now?" Leon checked each window.

"Yeah you see that Dodge Challenger parked further down on the right? That's surveillance. They haven't seen me though, don't worry."

"Oh, thanks Vincent, I can relax now," he scoffed. *01:49* read his watch.

"Okay so I watched him go in with some two foot rake who looks like he's just back from Chernobyl, and not a fucking care in the world as to how obvious they stood out. But it was just two of them. The gate is locked by a code and the CCTV sits up on the post there so I've parked back-"

"Vincent," interrupted Leon "have you thought this through?"

"What do you mean? Course I fucking-"

"Tell me your plan."

Vincent reached across Leon's seat and pulled open the glovebox. A six inch Colt Python and an IMI Desert Eagle dropped down.

"So, you're an assassin now?" asked Leon.

"Don't give me that shit, we've all done what we had to plenty of times over. At the end of the day, it's you or them. I don't ever trust the police to do their jobs. And I'm not waiting for the next time I buy my corn-flakes to bump into these psychopaths. Now I'm going in there. I'm going to end this and you will thank me - that dead girl's mother will thank me."

"Have you even thought about a getaway?"

"That's why you're here," Vincent said resting his hand on Leon's shoulder, "all you have to do is drive."

"Drive where? Into the police waiting for us? You don't even know how to get past surveillance, never mind how many guys are inside that place or the lay-out, and the clock is ticking. I told you I wanted no part in this anymore," Leon raised his voice.

"Yeah well I'm neck fucking deep in it and you owe me."

"I owe you?" Leon asked incredulous and seized Vincent by the collar.

"As my best friend," he shrugged like a sheep, "these cunts sliced me up and left me for dead. One last time. Will you help me? Remember, if we die, we die right. And this is right. Forget about me, these people are abducting pregnant teenagers and killing them in front of us. Be a hero."

"I can't be a part of this Vincent. I'm sorry."

"We've been brothers for life. This is just another episode. And whatever shit comes your way in the future, like always I got you too."

Leon ran his fingers through his hair, threatening to pull it out.

"This is not my life anymore," he said to himself.

Vincent sat back in his seat and gave up arguing, simply nodding to his own thoughts. "Well, I'm going in," he announced, "but first, I gotta make a call."

"What?"

"Hello, uhhh I need to report a sighting of the wanted murderer Franco Egan," Vincent talked to the police with over enunciation, trying to sound white and educated, "yes I'm 100% sure it's him, with the tribal tattoos on his face. I have spotted him on East 4th Street and he appears to be following a young girl... Okay thank you, please come quick."

They watched the surveillance in pregnant silence, and to Vincent's delight, the plan worked. The Dodge on lookout sped away from the street almost as fast as they could duck for cover.

Vincent turned to Leon all smug, then remembered

to be disappointed, saying, "4th Street is just a few blocks away but goes for miles, I reckon we have about twenty minutes. But you just wait here and play on your phone."

From under a rug in the back seat, Vincent grabbed a sawed-off shotgun and threw the strap over his shoulder as he jumped out of the car, pausing for a final shake of the head at Leon. With a trailing prosthetic leg, he staggered towards the barricades and flung a pistol out of his jacket to shoot the camera above the gate. The bang of the gun reverberated through the sleeping estate. The crash of falling glass followed. Leon watched him climb the railings with grating teeth. Somehow, he managed to sling his body over the barrier. He struggled to stick the landing but after a stumble his feet shelled the concrete, as he hobbled around the corner of the building - out of sight.

Leon scrambled across the car into the driver's seat - slamming the driver's door shut. He watched the still factory grounds unblinking, with all other senses tingling, waiting for something.

01:53 read the dashboard clock.

Five minutes, that's it and I'm gone, he thought. Sixty seconds of hyper adrenaline passed before he caved and opened the door to hostile air. Conflicted, it felt like gravity increased tenfold, holding his body from moving forward. Like a valve exploding, his will overcame fear as he dashed toward the barricades. He landed over the bars heavily and ready – but still nothing, no voices, no cries or sounds of a struggle. Just the gentle wind drying the sweat on his skin.

 Leon harried against the side of factory building, shuttering along the wall. A shattered window stood out further down and Leon crept his head around. Only chunks of wood and broken breeze blocks lay inside. Feet first he climbed into the room, tearing his sweatshirt on the broken glass but landing gently. Above the slow crunching of rubble pervaded a voice - in fact two - in muffled conversation. Leon followed their echoes, careful to avoid any standing objects. He walked tall and tread lightly along the corridors of falling dust, grazing his fingers along the dirt plastered walls for balance. The rising voices let him know he was winning the maze.

 At the end of corridor Leon poked his head around the corner. His heart skipped a beat seeing Vincent crouched behind the adjacent wall. When he finally saw Leon, his eyeballs jumped out of their sockets, but he settled down to give Leon a nod and his usual creepy smile. The voices were loud and clear:

 "She was screaming no, no, no, I have a family. And you're in a fucking bar alone at 2AM on a weekday? The kid probably won't even miss you darling," yapped Nichols.

 "Pretty much asking for it. Anyway, do we have any steak?"

 "What is it with you and fucking food?"

 They couldn't have been more than twenty metres away. Leon and Vincent stood either side of the open doorway, waiting for each other to give the signal to charge, when a toilet flushed behind them. In synchronisation, they craned their heads around toward the toilet door, then back at themselves in slow motion. Vincent's jaw dropped and his body froze. Leon pushed off the wall and ran toward the toilet. The door was ajar before he front kicked it back.

"What the fuck?" drawled a confused Franco inside.

Leon lay flat on the wall adjoined to the toilet. The door flew open and smacked against the other side. A silver Glock thrust out. Leon grabbed the gun and smashed Franco's hand against the wall, firing wild bullets as the gun fell free. Before his ears stopped ringing a huge fist cracked Leon's jaw. Laid out on his back he beheld the monster Franco, with raging veins pulsating like endless roots.

Leon sprung to his feet and charged towards the beast, wrestling him back into the toilet. Their bodies pummelled the mirror and shattered glass to the volley of gunfire outside. Franco grappled Leon's head beneath his fat belly, and with his arms locked under Leon's neck choked him. Leon felt his airways collapse instantly, swallowing empty air. Blue, pink splotches clouded his vision. Then he was barely there at all, watching his world fade away like it was someone else's life.

With his last conscious breath Leon slipped his hand between Franco's grip and yanked his head free. In a mist of delirium he head-butted Franco's chin and watched the beast crumble under his own weight. From the broken mirror Leon grasped a jagged piece and rammed it through Franco's carotid artery. A bloody waterfall spurt over Leon and he watched Franco collapse like a sack of shit. But for the fallen beasts gargling, quiet returned, and Leon looked around at what he had done. Footsteps ran behind him - he turned with the knife ready.

"Woah," said Vincent, throwing his arms up in surrender.

"Woah shit," yelled Vincent, "fucking yes," he thrust his fist at Franco drowning in blood, "choke on that you son of a bitch and know hell awaits."

Vincent slapped his hand on Leon's shoulder, "We have to go, wipe the blood off your face," he said.

Vincent remembered to destroy the CCTV but by the time they were ready to leave, and just as Leon's heart was slowing, the surveillance had returned.

"Fuck," whispered Vincent, peering between blinds.

"Follow me," said Leon.

He led the way out of a broken window on the far side of the building and they helped each other over the back wall, strolling round to the front again like kings of the manor, with Vincent holding Franco's cross earring as a souvenir. Leon threw his stained sweater in the trunk of the car, and they drove away peacefully into the night, but Leon wasn't celebrating.

"Where did the other guys go?" Leon asked sternly.

"They scurried away like rats after the first few shots," Vincent cackled.

"Why?"

"Because they're rats. And because I shot this little

bastard in the hand – God did he scream like a bitch. And hey," said Vincent, becoming sincere, "thank you man, really."

Leon kept his focus on the road.

"Hey," said Vincent, shaking Leon, "we fucking got them, man."

Leon watched Vincent dance in his seat and was happy for him to have his moment, but the wheels were set in motion to somewhere else, and the falling dominoes were already chasing them.

"Everyone in this van will hit the front," Denzel lead the SWAT team.

The armoured raid vehicle shot through the highway, shaking the windows and Max's nerve.

"Max you're my observer."

"Yes sir," she battle cried.

"Joe, you're my scout."

Max pulled body armour over her head with white fingertips. Fidgeted with the position of night vision goggles on her head. Stopped the assault rifle rattling between her knees.

"I want everybody air fucking tight on this," said Denzel, "focus. There may be hostages."

An emergency call interrupted his speech. Denzel swallowed his rehearsed words and pressed the headphone into his ear to hear clearly.

"There have been reports of gunfire at your destination. Please proceed as fast as possible and show caution."

"Understood," Denzel called back, "ETA of five minutes. Over and out."

"Be prepared for multiple hostiles and return fire," he yelled, "get your night vision on we're going in dark. And soon."

All lights in the vehicle were switched off and Max scrambled for her goggles, entering a world made of green pixels. In front of her, Joe sat like a statue with his head down in the brief calm before the storm.

"This is Detective Denzel Brooks, what are our eyes in the sky seeing?"

"Drones are detecting no activity outside the premises, with possible blood splatters inside. We recommend a window entry south of the property."

With the vehicle's tyres still rolling they stormed the building behind a flashbang. Trails of blood left by fingers passed Max at the door. She followed in a snake formation, careful not to get lost in the vague shapes. She took her area of responsibility, covering each corner. The spattered blood became footprints before her feet soon dipped into a pool.

"Hold your position."

Max stopped and felt herself sinking. The gun's light hit Franco Egan's face. Dead to the blinding torch, with his tattoos drowned in blood he hosted dinner for insects. Max got lost in the still life.

"Max confirm the pulse."

She bent down keeping her breathing away from the mess, pointlessly placing two fingers on his neck above the gaping gash.

"Dead," she whispered.

"What?"

"Target is dead," she said.

"Okay move along we secure the building."

With impeccable procedure they cleared the rest of the place out, finding only empty rounds and dirt, chasing shadows.

GET OUT

Vincent and Leon stood under murky street lights in the eclipse of night. They argued making too much noise, like the singing crickets around them, vulnerable to predators. And Leon felt their approach.

"You gotta get out, Vincent," demanded Leon.

Vincent tried averting his attention elsewhere, looking anywhere but into Leon's eyes. So he kept stepping back into Vincent's path.

"I said, you gotta get out of this state now," he yelled, holding Vincent by the scruff of his neck.

"What do you mean? Why?" Vincent shot back with false ire.

"You know exactly why."

"Who did this?" posed Donnie, standing over the light of fire.

The flames revealed fresh carvings on his face, slashed down his right eye and across his cheek. Self-inflicted, as his new war paint. At his feet, Nichol's clothes from the battle with Vincent turned to ashes.

"I don't know, I didn't see them properly," Henry mumbled at the ground.

"Too fast running away weren't you, Henry?"

Donnie turned his sight to Nichols, who knelt before him in the forest. Nichols kept his head like a distressed dog and held his bandaged hand.

"I think it was a guy we robbed a few months ago."

"Interesting," announced Donnie, "looks like you'll get another chance to introduce yourself, Henry."

"They saw your face and they will hunt you down," Leon added weight to his words and shoved Vincent.

Vincent threw him back, "You think I'm not ready?" he shouted out of grinding teeth.

They wrestled each other like two fools in a drunken bar.

"I know you're not," Leon's sober words overcame Vincent.

"So, what, what do you want me to do?" Vincent stuttered.

"I want you to leave the state and keep going."

"But what about you?"

"So you just left Franco there to die?" asked Donnie.

"Yes, we're sorry."

"This time your cowardice has paid off," Donnie said biting his lip, "they've found their murderer. Franco made many mistakes and almost got us all caught too soon. Why do you think I wasn't around for the last few days? Huh? Because I'm not that stupid. And I watched your pathetic performance through a camera link on my laptop."

 Henry watched blood trickle down Donnie's lip, afraid of his state of mind.

 "The police will be distracted by Franco's killer. But we can't have them forgetting about us now, can we? I want you to send a gift to one of the cops."

 "Don't worry about me, they didn't see my face," said Leon letting Vincent go, "I'll come meet you," he lied.

 Vincent shook his head, "Let go of that bitch man."

 Leon throttled Vincent. "Don't you fucking talk about her, don't you fucking talk about her," he screamed losing control.

TICK TOCK

17th AUGUST

Tick tock.

The eye on the wall stared down. Tick tock, the dark hand beat past six. Leon waited in his apartment, laying back on the armchair, flicking between the clock and his phone. His thumb hovered over Ellie's name, but he turned off the cell instead.

Over to the fridge he strolled, opening-closing the door before he even really looked inside. He paced into the bedroom. Out of the draw he held the handgun, watching the warped reflection of his face in the silver again, feeling a little closer to self-destructing. Leon dropped the gun and got back in his armchair, stuck in the twilight zone.

His phone buzzed: *(323) 324-4152 calling.*

Not recognising the number, he answered the phone silently.

"Hello," spoke a woman he still didn't know, "is this a relative of Mrs Bridget Fields? Hello?"

"Yes?"

"We found your name and number as an emergency contact for Mrs Fields, is this a good time to talk?"

"Sure," said Leon blasé.

"Mrs Fields has had a fall at the nursing home, and is currently in the California Hospital Medical Centre."

"Okay," his voice toughened.

"Do you know where it is?" she added tenderly.

"Yes, thank you."

"Okay, just so you know she's not in the best way."

"Thanks for letting me know," said Leon.

"Okay. I'm so sorry... Anything else you need call us. Okay bye," she said too eager.

Leon left for the hospital right away but got caught in traffic.

"Come on," he pleaded and punched the wheel.

The ant line seemed endless, but in a blur of anxiety he was soon climbing the hospital steps, battling his way through the queues.

"A fractured vertebrate and tibia. Four broken ribs, with some internal bleeding. There are also some minor bruises to the skull, but it was the severity of the breaks, coupled with her osteoporosis that meant we had to operate straight away. We do not usually like to operate when a patient has dementia as the anaesthetics can have a detrimental effect which they may not recover from. But, the most pressing issue is the infection she has developed post-surgery. We do not believe in her weakened state, that she will be able to fight it. We cannot say how long exactly we expect her to keep fighting, but she may not make it through the night," said the fledgling Doctor, struggling to keep cool. Flushed skin and blinking eyes gave him away. Just a nice Middle-Eastern boy doing his parents proud, thought Leon, probably straight out of med school. Still un-callused. Too young.

Leon stood beside the hospital bed that she rest in, and to his naked eyes swore her body already lay breathless. Still as wax, she slept with her arms folded and her mouth open to the heavens. The florescent light revealed features more ravaged than ever, leaving her like a caricature, drawn by her Reaper. Her bald eyebrows made for a blank face - the virtue of her true self had already passed. All that was left was her shell. Leon barely recognised it.

He ran his fingers through the wrinkles of her purple skin, deep like dried up rivers. And through the hair which sprouted in clumps on her head, letting the dry skin spread over his fingertips. Back and forth softly - to let himself know as much as her, that he was still there. She let out a groan and a splutter of her lips.

"It's me, Leon," he assured her.

Her eyelids battled to open, collapsing as they made it halfway but still trying.

"Where is my Leon?" her words slurred.

He held her hand, and said, "Right beside you."

"Right beside me," she said squeezing his hand, "right beside me. Right beside me. Right beside me," she cried holding onto memories of him.

Leon kept her hand in his and stayed with her throughout the night, until she choked her last breath and her hand let go.

He kissed her on the forehead - like she used to when he was a kid - and looked back through the open door one last time, as it closed too soon.

As he stepped out of the hospital into the fresh morning air, Leon stopped to view the lives around him. They buried their heads in phones with apathy to him and scurried along unaware of his existence. *06:49* read his watch. Tick tock. Their feet beat against the concrete. Litter swirled in his face. The cool breeze shivered his bones. And yet, like a ray of light from the night sky, this dawn awoke Leon from the solitude of his mind. Relief. Misery. Guilt. It mused his battling thoughts.

He wandered along the pavements, watching children kick a can across the road, feeling the shake of a plane above, breathing in polluted air that never tasted so good. For no real reason, just because he could. Just because they were real, and he was there. Leon had awoken from his daydream, and felt like he was the one directing life for the first time in a while.

Leon gripped the wheel of his car, and the veins on his hand pulsed slowly. For how many hours he lost count, but he drove. Out on the open highways with the windows down. The passing shapes carried him to distant thoughts, once suppressed, now free.

He drove past O'*Grady's* bar, where he met up with Vincent all those months ago. Its retro white italics couldn't have looked shabbier in the daylight. One beer can't hurt, he thought, leaving the car by the curb.

The creaking wooden doors released welcome chatter. On his usual stool at the bar, he didn't even bother checking himself in the mirror, only one thing mattered.

"Budweiser please pal."

"Here you go," Gerry grunted.

Whacked down on the bar top was just what he needed. Condensation cold. Props to Captain Blackbeard, he thought, throwing him a lazy salute. Just as he was about to taste the sweet sip of a Bud, a hand rest on his neck. In the mirror, Dr Radford beamed over his shoulder.

"How are you doing, kid?" shouted the Dr heartily.

"I'm good. I'm good," he said struggling to hear him.

"I'm sitting over here, come over and join me?"

Leon considered it.

"Come on, come on," he waved Leon over.

"Sure."

Leon followed him into a quieter corner, away from the jukebox playing Born to Run and the rowdy men huddled below the television, to a wooden cubicle. They sat facing each other across the table, with Leon already feeling like he was laying back in a psychiatrist's office.

"Cheers," declared Dr Radford, clinking his pint against Leon's.

"Cheers."

"I didn't expect to see you in an old timers bar like this," said the Dr.

"I didn't expect to see you drinking on a school day."

"But it's Saturday?" the Dr laughed.

"Oh right yeah, sorry," Leon laughed along, "one beer in and I don't know what day it is."

"But okay it is only early evening, and I may have a little work tomorrow I'll give you that, but the wife is at pilates and if you had seen me try pilates you would know the best place for me is here."

Dr Radford lurched forward with his elbows on the table, "So, tell me kid, how you been?"

"Well," said Leon falling back, "me and Ellie broke up the other week, my grandma died today and tomorrow I'll still be drunk, that's all I've summarised so far."

"Fuck," uttered Dr Radford, left gawping, "and here I am smiling and laughing."

"It's okay."

"No it's not," the Dr fought back. Focused, he said, "I'm sorry Leon. I didn't know about your grandma because I left the Clinic last week. But what I do know, is that she was a wonderfully vibrant woman. I mean, she definitely loved you, and she didn't half make me laugh," he chuckled, "I remember, the ringtone went off on my phone once and she was up jigging around dancing before the second beat. Guns N' Roses. She was enjoying it so much I didn't even answer the call."

"Thank you doc," Leon half-smiled, "I mean Bob."

"Finally, we get a Bob," he exclaimed.

"I thought I'd mix it up, but tell me, why did you leave the hospital?"

"Oh," jumped Dr Radford's voice, and the question made him fidget, "it just wasn't working out in the end. Truth is, I think I just need a break. You know? I wasn't sure I was helping people anymore."

"Well, no one could have helped my grandma. I always found it strange she was in the study, actually. But I can say you were a great help to Ellie."

"Thank you, I appreciate it. But um, there was plenty I couldn't save, unfortunately…"

The Dr didn't fight his tearing eyes. He cried stone faced but smiled for Leon's benefit.

"I'm sorry, it's actually my daughter's birthday. Would have been about Ellie's age now, actually. I'm sorry to hear about you and Ellie breaking up too, she told me wonderful things about your relationship," Dr Radford tried to change the subject.

"What happened to your daughter?" said Leon.

Dr Radford dithered, "She, she died of pneumonia. Not long after her fourth birthday."

"I'm sorry."

The Dr's eyes drifted past him.

"It's okay," Dr Radford said flapping his hand, "it's been eighteen years. But," his voice wavered, "me and the wife Jean can't really face each other on Hayley's anniversaries. Sorry again, here I am babbling on like you're my shrink when it's your grandma who has died."

"You know I used to imagine myself talking to shrinks," spoke Leon, "filling in what they would say to me. I suppose you would have a lot to say about that. What do you reckon?"

"Well," he said, "it's always good to question yourself. As they say, the unexamined life is not worth living."

"Do people *really* say that?" joked Leon.

"Nah just a guy called Socrates in about 400BC. Philosophy is probably the reason I joined the hospital's study on suicide actually. You heard of Albert Camus?"

"The ginger WWE wrestler?"

"Close," laughed Dr Radford, "he was a famous French writer from the early 20th century. And he believed in the end, our existence needed to conquer one proposition: that of suicide. With there being just two solutions available to us. Embrace life's absurdity, or if it becomes too much, kill ourselves. His hero of absurdity was Sisyphus, the great Greek myth, condemned by the Gods for eternity to roll a stone up a hill - only for it to fall back again as he reached the top. You probably heard of him, right?"

"Um sure. Despite his fate," said, Leon, taking over the story, "Sisyphus chose to go back down the hill, and push the rock all the way up again. Every time, forever."

"Right," rejoiced Dr Radford, "so, I wanted to talk to people that felt like they only had those two choices. Get an in-depth understanding of why they felt like giving up, give them a hand pushing the rock, and I guess convince them there is a mountain top after all."

"But, is there a mountain top?"

"Does it matter, if you're happy believing there is an end?"

The humour in the air expired, and they were just two sad men in a bar, searching for answers.

"So do you believe in God?" asked Leon to fill the silence.

"Yes," affirmed Dr Radford.

"Even after your daughter?"

"Even after my daughter."

Dr Radford joined Leon in slouching back on the bench, taking a moment to breathe it all in. The smoke travelling down the bar and the damp air he'd tasted more times than home dinners.

"After all this time," he exhaled, "you know, with all the lost memories of my daughter I could've written a wonderful story. Full of happiness, and second chances. But I can only paint the outlines, and barely remember her smile on her birthday or the feeling I felt when she was born. I know that the fading of these thoughts is really a blessing, saving me from suffering forever. But what is this presence? A shitty simple watercolour of moments crossing over each other, no picture of ourselves ever complete. Just travelling down a road we don't know, with only our washed-out memories to remind us of who we really are. I am forgetting what it feels like to be me, with each detail of my daughter lost in time – But sure kid, I still believe."

"That could just be the beer talking doc, it is good stuff," said Leon, taken aback.

"Maybe," Dr Radford conceded, "maybe. Speaking of which you're slacking son."

"But," Leon considered his words "Bob, sorry I don't know how to phrase this differently, but, if there is a God, why did he take your daughter?"

The Dr met the question like he had been awaiting it his whole life.

"And why has he let countless other innocent die throughout history? From disease, war, and famine? To the unlucky guy who walked the same way to work for ten years, but didn't look left on one morning. Yes, I understand the question. But you know people have been writing answers to the problem of evil for thousands of years. I don't have anything profound to say. There's multiple theodicies with strong arguments, but none of them seem good enough or fair, when it is our loved one or ourselves that are the victim. But we speak of God as though he were a man, and a separate being, with a consciousness that decides what is justice for each man, woman, and their pet. These are all human projections. God is good? God is just a word we chose for something greater than ourselves. But God is everything to me. And if I am to believe in a purpose greater than my own life, I cannot think only about my own perception. And when you look at good and evil on a larger scale, between life and the world. Good is winning, right? And that's something to believe in. To be honest, I have to."

"But what good do you see?" asked Leon, "What purpose? Like any animal, we kill, we eat, we reproduce and die. As you said, anything else is a projection Bob, a pacifier to our self-awareness of how trivial we are."

"Did you see your grandma's purpose in life as to merely eat, drink and reproduce, then slowly decay until death?" countered Dr Radford.

"That's what she did," said Leon.

"But what of her love for you and her family? Did that not count for something?"

"What does it count for," said Leon, "when ultimately it could not stop her dying?"

"You know," said Dr Radford, "you know. Don't think you fool me. You've felt it."

"Sure."

"You're damn right sure," Dr Radford said hitting his pint glass on the table, "and you're right, human nature is basic preservation of their own life. But one day, you'll sacrifice the priority of your life for another and find fulfilment. And once you do, you'll discover that this world is full of paradoxes - then you will understand my choices."

The Dr ventured into the bottom of his pint glass, into *Alice and Wonderland* with his stories, thought Leon, before ascending to reality again like a bolt of lightning.

"Hey don't mind me son, I'm rambling," he spoke practising his normal demeanour, "truth is, I don't know shit beyond these four walls. I'm just reaching."

"I think you should be a priest," spoke a bewildered but impressed Leon.

"Nah they're more corrupt than anyone, I think I'll stick to being a failed Doctor thanks," he laughed desperately, "and look forward to my beers, tacos and becoming too senile to care about it all."

"That's a philosophy I can believe in. Do you know where the phrase, eat, sleep and be merry for tomorrow we die comes from? The Bible. It's about the only thing I can quote from the book, but my point is, that was yesterday. And today we're still alive and we all want to live for bigger dreams. Like Ellie who needed to be a model or like my grandma who tortured herself so much trying to be better than a cleaner. The trouble is, if you chase your dreams and don't succeed, they begin to follow you in life. They'll haunt you. And then you almost desperately need an afterlife for it all to be okay again, you know? That's why I just try to be in the here and now."

"Well cheers to that happy thought," Dr Radford said trying to drink from his empty glass.

"To your daughter," Leon raised his bottle.

To thank him, Dr Radford lifted one last glimmer of hope in his face, smiling with crow's feet larger than the tracks of his tears.

"To your grandma."

GOODBYE

Denzel bobbed his head to Justin Bieber's one note melody, parting traffic at 60 mph.

"Why are we listening to this?" moaned Max, fighting over the car stereo.

"I thought you'd like it," he said feeling the rhythm.

"No, this is what my niece would like," she answered.

What Max kept secret, was that she was resisting the urge to sing.

"Well, you sound just like my son."

Denzel turned the music down to talk clearly.

"At least he has good taste."

They had spent hours not doing much detective work at all. First, answering questions about Franco Egan's death to the powers that be. And secondly, chasing their tails to make themselves look busy with the case. Truth is, following the raid they didn't know where to turn. So Denzel was making extra effort to lift the mood.

That's not to say there wasn't a few surprises from the investigation. Nobody else was discovered in the building, but they did find a second person's DNA on the glass which severed Franco's carotid artery. They just didn't know it was Leon's.

As for fingerprints, they found a few, but like the DNA they didn't have any matches to their files, and so the case felt like a waiting game for now. Plus, if any more missing persons became attached to the case, Denzel was sure the FBI would take over soon anyway.

"So how old is your son?" asked Max.

"He's thirty four, at 18:21 today."

"Holy shit Denzel, then how old are you?" Max's jaw hit the floor.

"I'll have you know, I'm fifty two."

"Wow, so you were a father quite young then?" Max asked with her thinking face on, trying to do the math.

"Yes indeed, I was just eighteen and finishing high school when my childhood sweetheart surprised me. Best surprise of my life though. But damn, thirty four years ago? It's true what they say, life is what happens when you're busy making other plans. I'm still planning to retire at forty to the Bahamas," Denzel said scratching an imaginary itch on his chin.

"Damn I still can't imagine being responsible enough to have kids and I'm twenty seven."

"Oh don't be silly, you would make a great mother."

Denzel felt the friendship he'd been working at.

"Ah, don't," said Max, and the mood fell.

"What's Alicia like anyway? I can't believe I've never met her?"

"Umm, she's tall and Hispanic like me. But think of a

better tan, better curly hair, some cool tattoos and is a saint who works all night shifts as a nurse at a children's hospital," Max said insecurely.

"Sounds like a catch, so when you getting married?"

She thought about making something up, but her mouth didn't waste any time, "Alicia told me she's moving out last week."

"Oh shit," said Denzel, "after how hard you've been trying? That's a real kick in the face."

"Thank you, for your comforting words."

"I mean, shit," he started again in a calmer register, "remember, I've been married for over thirty years, so I can't remember that much about breakups, but..." Denzel didn't have a 'but' ready to say.

"...But I can just bury myself in work and pretend it never happened?" Max finished the sentence.

"Hell no, you still cherish the good times, but there's plenty more fish in the pond, right?"

"You're really bad at this Denzel."

"I know I'm going to stop now."

They broke the pretend awkwardness with a peek across the car at each other, trying not to laugh first.

"Joking aside, I do appreciate all the help you give me," said Max, "honest."

"No problem at all, you're teaching me new things too."

"Like patience?" joked Max.

"Hell yeah," he laughed.

Denzel drove into his suburban neighbourhood of Culver City. In all the commotion at work, he forgot he was supposed to be home earlier today for his son's birthday and a family dinner. For once, he would even let Max drive the department's car back to the station.

"Listen," called Denzel, as thoughts of work returned to him, "I know I'm always saying we have to try harder and we're going catch them, and this and that, but sometimes you don't get the bad guy. And that's okay. Our real lives are still waiting for us. Sometimes you don't get to be the hero, it's somebody else's turn."

Blunt as a hammer, Max said, "We're going to catch them."

Denzel's thoughts stopped in their tracks and he gave in happily to the notion, "Okay yes we are."

He didn't get far up his driveway before hearing Max shout, "Denzel," from the curb.

"Thanks for saying goodbye," she said sarcastically.

He swivelled on a dime and said, "Goodbye," with a jovial royal wave.

Max hoped this was the beginning of a new chapter, with Alicia in her life or not. Denzel was the friend she needed right now, even if he was super uncool. She even imagined coming over for dinner next time.

And then that future died.

Like the flick of a switch, Denzel shut the front door and the building ignited out of nothing, exploding into a ball of fire, spreading like waves.

The blast swept the car away and Max rolled in glass. She had seen only a flash of light but she wasn't really there. Her mind was with Denzel, and she had only tears to douse the flames.

SLIDING DOORS

Leon stumbled out of the Pontiac into a sweltering night, torturously humid, but he didn't give a shit - still drunk from his all-day session with Dr Radford. He parked in his normal space by the corner and slapped his fake permit on the windshield.

Wait. Whose car is that? He thought. Leon was inebriated but still paranoid enough about Vincent's attackers to notice. He kept a check on all the vehicles regularly parked here, but six rows along he spotted an unfamiliar Ford Ranger – covered in dust.

Leon gave the car the benefit of the doubt but kept thinking about its presence in the lift. Stood outside his apartment the black door remained unblinking to his stare. Leon lurked like a ghost in the shadows of the stairwell. Has it always been like that? He thought, noticing the doorknob hanging crooked. His feet backed away from the door. Instead, he knocked on Linda's apartment at the floor below. She opened the door sleepy-eyed, in her dressing gown and hair net.

"Oh hey?" Linda said bemused.

Using the powers of liquid confidence, he gave his best pretend-to-be-normal performance.

"Sorry to bother you, Linda. I've locked myself out, and I'm just going to climb up from your balcony, if that's okay?"

"Oh," she said struggling to wake up or care, "that seems a bit dangerous?"

"Oh no, no, I'm actually an experienced rock climber. In free climbing as well – haven't used a harness since I was a boy. I wouldn't put you in this position if there was any problem. It will take me less than a minute, I promise."

Leon made his way in before she could counter him, treading over Lego and heading straight through to the balcony. The sliding door shut on Leon. Inside, her kid Lucian peeked his head out from under the dining table, giving Leon the stink eye. He shot Lucian a military salute goodbye and the kid waved back. Feeling like a circus performer, Leon climbed up onto the balcony rail, balancing on the tips of his toes. In a single spring, he leapt and caught the bars above. And slipped. Only five clammy fingers clung onto the damp bars. One hand at a time, he yanked himself up, careful not to look down at the sixty feet drop. With his head just above the platform he peered beneath the curtain: no shoes.

The wind tried to loosen his grip again but he slung himself over the railing, just in time. Beneath the curtain of the balcony door black boots stepped towards him. Leon's heart raced. His fist clenched. The boots stepped away. About to climb back down Leon stopped. Someone was knocking on his front door.

Two sets of feet scampered along the carpet.

Don't be Linda, thought Leon. He heard her muffled voice. Fuck. Inch by inch, he silently glided open the balcony door and scanned the room through a slit in the curtain. It was them – the gang from the warehouse. The long haired ginger guy and the two foot rat-face that Vincent described. They'd found him. But they hadn't seen him yet, he thought. With their backs to Leon, they loomed over the half-opened front door with their hidden shotguns cocked.

"Is Leon here?" Linda asked.

"Oh yeah, he's just in the toilet. Can we take a message?" answered Henry, with a fake English accent.

Leon slipped behind them into the bedroom.

"No that's okay, just checking he got in all right," he heard Linda say.

Leon took the Browning Hi Power from his draw and loaded the gun.

"We'll let him know you stopped by," said Henry, and the door slammed shut.

"Now she's seen our fucking faces," Nichols whispered angrily.

"No matter we'll come for her after," said Henry.

"And what did she mean, get in okay? You think something's up?"

"Fuck knows, who cares, we just need to wait."

Leon hid against the bedroom wall, beside the open door to the living room and entrance. He could feel the proximity of their voices, standing within touching distance of the bedroom door, drawing closer. Many times Leon had reconciled himself to a futile fate, or at least said the words in his mind. Though he had never truly felt despair until this moment. There was no happy ending for him. There could never have been.

But there was no turning back now.

In one unfaltering movement Leon spun through the open door and shot Nichols through the back of his head. His skull shattered like a watermelon. His blood paint splattered the white walls.

Leon felt Henry's return fire before he'd even heard the gun go off. His left shoulder pulsed like it was about to burst. In a reflex action he shot back and pierced Henry's neck. Like a fool, Henry dropped his gun to hold the wound. Instantly - with eyes like a deer in the headlights - Henry scrambled for his shotgun on the ground. Reduced to the animal he was, scampering on all fours, Leon duly shot him in the back as he crawled.

By his hair, Leon flung Henry belly up.

"You fucking cunt," croaked Henry, spitting, gargling and gushing blood, flooding the apartment.

Leon stood over him and asked, "Was it really worth it?"

He held the gun at Henry's forehead and his eyes rolled wide.

"You're going to fucking die," snarled Henry.

"But you first."

"He's going to get you," sang Henry.

"Who?"

Henry cackled between the splutters of blood and

strained to sit up – Leon cocked the gun and he halted.

"You don't even have a fucking clue, do you?" whispered Henry in gleeful awe.

"Who?" shouted Leon.

"You'll find out soon," Henry sang the next verse.

"Who?" Leon screamed louder.

"And so will the people you love."

Leon pulled the trigger.

The sea of blood flowed onto his boots and Leon looked around at the two bodies resting dead. And yet it still wasn't the end. He took cartridges of bullets from his draw and filled his pockets for whoever came next.

When he walked out into the eerily quiet corridor Leon had expected people to be waiting. Maybe even police. But the only human he saw was a child peering out from a neighbour's door ajar. In a face of shadow the boy was afraid of him, with his haunted stare fixed on Leon's bloody clothes. The door slammed shut when he saw Leon had spotted him. A lone ranger, Leon walked into the elevator as an actor in his own life, and the doors slid shut on him once more.

DEAD MAN'S EYE

The stream rippled through channels, trickling in the morning breeze. Sunlight bounced off the water evanescently, as Leon sat in his car underneath a bridge, watching the sunrise over the drainage system. Out of the car door, he bled drops into the water, enjoying the halcyon hours, before more rivers of blood.

Last time he checked the time was 5AM something. Seven hours had passed since he murdered those men at his apartment. And for only about thirty minutes, he had been able to sleep against the headrest. As he woke repeatedly, back in the midst of the fight. The jolt of his waking body pulsated the wound still deep in his shoulder, inside the speckled holes left by the shotgun. Luckily, most of the pellets grazed him. He scraped out what remained, and with strapping the bleeding had dried for now.

Twice he had attempted to call Ellie already this morning.

Leon squirmed his hips - trying not to disturb his shoulder - whilst reaching for the cell in his pocket. The phone fell into his waiting hand and he dialled Ellie's name again. Except for this time, her phone answered.

"Well I guess this saves me calling you," a hoarse voice cut.

Leon's jaw clenched shut, saying nothing.

"Don't you recognise me? It's your old pal, Donnie."

"Where is Ellie?"

"I thought you might ask that," said Donnie, "scream for me princess."

"Help me please help me," Ellie cried with every fibre.

"What have you done to her?" Leon tried to ask composed.

"You went under my radar Leon. I didn't even know you had a name, you just turned up at meetings and had a good stare. It's always the quiet ones, hey?"

"What have you done to her?" Leon raged.

"Oh don't worry, just a few new scars, a couple happy memories to remember me by."

"You're going to die," said Leon, his hand near crushing the phone.

"Well, who wants to live forever?" preached Donnie, "And I suppose you are going to be the one to kill me?"

"I am going to kill you."

"You should feel lucky she's not in pieces," Donnie's voice quickened, "I heard what you did to my guys."

"And I'm going to do the same to you."

"A-ha ha ha ha ha," Donnie cackled like a hyena, "that's the spirit. Because I want you to come save her."

"Where?"

"Well call me poetic, but I fancy another showdown

in an abandoned building. Come to 615 off East 61st Street. I even made it close for you. But bear in mind, if you call the cops – I slit her throat. If you bring anyone else – I saw her fucking head off. If you do both, well, you get the picture. You're doing so well being the hero by yourself, don't ruin it now."

"Like I said, it's going to be just me that kills you," Leon swore.

"I gotta say, for such the hero it's a shame you couldn't save your grandma."

There was silence but for the trickling water.

"Oh did I not mention? It was me that killed her. Didn't take long for Vincent to tell me everything. Stubborn old bitch too hanging on like she did, it was a high window. In the end, I didn't even have to throw her, I just told her I'd kill you if she didn't jump. Not Leon please, she blubbered like a pathetic -"

Leon hung up but replayed the words over and over. He cried shaking the steering wheel until he ran out of breath, gasping for air with ineffable anger. Eyes closed, he fell into the hole before him. Lost in a vacuum. Falling pictures of his grandma dragged him down to despair. Only by the strength of his rage could Leon find the hidden steps, opening his eyes to the word, "Ellie."

He switched on the ignition and let the engine roar for all to hear. The Pontiac glided around the streets and flew along the highway. Ellie sat before his eyes on the first day he met her. A sad portrait the world fit perfectly around her. Square white dentures. His Nan smiled wildly.

How could he have not seen Donnie coming?

Leon saw the torture in his grandma's face, but he could not save her again.

"Help me please help me," Ellie's cry echoed.

As the car flew up the arching highway dawn's aurora crept over the hill's horizon. The sunlight hit Leon's eyes but he did not blink. Out of despair, he raced into the fire. But the sky was soon smirched into the warehouse. Another industrial estate. This time in South LA. In the centre of an empty parking lot was a twelve floor empty office block. Shattered windows were boarded with plywood propped up by broken bricks.

Like a battering ram, he charged the vehicle toward the desolate tower. The car skid on its brakes, halting inches from the entrance. Leon grasped the Browning from his jacket pocket and sprinted at the door. Once, twice, three times he kicked the door until it flew off its hinges. From the crashing wood ascended a dust cloud. The nozzle of the gun led the way through the mist. Leon's finger tightened on the trigger. Yet from the veiled shapes emerged no one. The lobby was deserted. Dust remained on the light switch - only Leon's breaths filled the room. He raced through the lobby to the stairwell. His heart beat even louder than his feet. With his back against the wall, he maximised his vision around the corners, tip-toeing up the steps. Bullets blew past his head. Broken tiles fell down on him. Leon jumped back around the corner.

"Are you ready to die?" sung Donnie.

In anger Leon stepped back into the firing line and shot in the direction of the noise – the rounds ricocheted off a bannister below Donnie's peeping head. He was just two floors above with his face newly decorated in slashes all over. He ran up the stairwell and Leon hunted him behind every step of the way. Bullets pin-balled off the shattering walls and they took turns to exchange fire with reckless abandonment, partners in the Devil's dance. Until a shot grazed Leon's thigh and he collapsed to his knees. They held their crouched positions, both hiding out of sight.

"You know you can't win," teased Donnie, "you must know that by now?"

With all his might Leon raised his wounded leg and got back on his feet.

"Tell me Leon, what keeps you moving forward?"

Leon anchored his mind to a single thought: saving Ellie. And with his slowing breaths he composed his senses.

"Is it pride? Love? Is it redemption?"

Leon fired blindly over the bannister.

"Oh it is, is it?" shrilled Donnie. He hung his head over the railings above and smiled with all his gums like a giddy child.

"You don't really think by killing me you're the good guy do you?" asked Donnie, "The only outcome today is one murderer killing another. Don't you forget that. You hold this anger for me because I cut up your best friend, killed your grandma, and I'm about to kill your girlfriend. Sure. Fair enough. But you killed three of my family too. And like you, I'm just actor and audience in my short scene, there are forces you cannot stop. I am just the end to your means. You chose me to be your nemesis. You're as culpable as anyone for how this will end."

Leon heard a door shut - Donnie had run through the 7th floor exit. Helter-skelter Leon chased him, barging through the swinging doors he stumbled into an empty corridor.

Donnie had turned its corner, waiting for him.

Leon knelt down beside the corner, and as expected Donnie returned. The rifle went off, but Leon arose beneath Donnie and they tussled for the gun. With the rifle as leverage he head-butted Donnie, splitting a chunk out of his nose. In return Donnie sprang a knife from his waist and dove it into Leon's chest. The rifle hit the ground.

Leon's rage wilted under the cold burning blade, so deep it froze his thoughts. But only for a second. They fought over the six inch knife nestled into Leon's flesh, holding hands, and writhing every atom to gain control. Their shadows like cave paintings of epic battles.

Donnie's snarl fell to a snigger under the rising tension. And in the knowledge Leon was overpowering him. The blade shuddered out of Leon's body, excruciatingly slow, before plunging into Donnie's own chest. With a fury that could shatter the circles of hell, Donnie shrieked and stumbled backwards.

Down at the blade and up at Leon, Donnie glared. In one swoop he tore the blade from his chest and held the knife up like a butcher mid swing, waiting for Leon's move, eerily tranquil. The slashes on Donnie's face were now lost in the melee of blood, dripping like melting wax.

Only half the blood was his own.

Leon could feel his body failing him. Whatever it takes, he swore.

Without fear, Leon stepped forward as Donnie swiped at him with the knife. Without thought, Leon side-stepped the blade and cracked Donnie in the jaw with a left hook. Ferociously Donnie swung the blade like an axe but Leon caught his flailing arm and booted him in the stomach. Donnie's body deflated with all the hot air kicked out of him. Doubled over he fled through the swinging doors behind them like a coward. Into the unknown Leon followed him.

In his mind's eye he got lost in Ellie's gaze on a summer night.

When Leon pushed open the swinging doors Ellie stood before him. With tears trembling off her bruised skin, begging Leon to save her. Her mouth and hands were taped shut as Donnie clinched her body, pressing the blade against her neck.

On Ellie's eyes Leon remained fixed, prisms to all their memories in this moment.

"Hand over the gun or she's dead," proclaimed Donnie.

"Hand her to me. And I will pass you the gun."

"You know how it works," teased Donnie, "lay the gun on the ground and step back now."

Leon tactically placed the Browning between them and stood back. Donnie leapt for the gun but his eagerness betrayed him, as Ellie's running feet kicked the piece away. She ran into Leon's arms and they fell into a sprint, escaping back into the corridors. Leon ripped the tape from her mouth and Ellie panted for oxygen to keep afoot. They tripped through empty workshops and offices searching for an exit, but the sound of Donnie chasing them grew.

"Here," said Leon, and they knelt behind a row of cupboards to hide.

"Leon I need to tell you something," whispered Ellie.

Leon kept his sights fixed around the cupboard's edge.

"Shh," he whispered.

She held his face defiantly and said, "I love you."

A lump of wood soared off the cupboard as bullets rained.

"I see you," echoed Donnie's voice.

"And I'm sorry," she whispered, "if this is it, I just want to say-"

Leon kissed Ellie and their minds shut out the chaos, sharing still darkness.

He listened to the twelfth round and knew what to do. Donnie's footsteps crept closer. It was time. He rose to accept the bullet, right through his chest but with his stride unbroken. Hearing the gun click without fire, cold sweat melted Donnie's nefarious face to fear. He gawped at Leon with a dead man's eye at the ghost of all his sins.

Leon clasped Donnie's throat and watched his life expire. Repeatedly Donnie tried to beat his hands away, but Leon was too strong. They fell together, and he held him down until Donnie's departed eyes glazed over. And in his reflection, Leon watched himself collapse, slipping out of consciousness.

> Wild lights danced in the dark, red, blue and
> white
>
> As stars fell like dandelions in spring
>
> His mad dreams fought with waking life to-
> night
>
> Time's hand stroked his pale skin, cold, wise
> and light
>
> As blood fell from he who would be crowned
> king
>
> Wild lights danced in the dark, red, blue and
> white
>
> Death's call hung up on him, out of the fight
>
> As masks fall and the drunk audience sing
>
> His mad dreams fought with waking life to-
> night

Father please save me now, with all your
  might

As you hold my sinful soul by a string

Wild lights danced in the dark, red, blue and
  white

Ellie's eyes were evanescently bright

Wild lights danced in the dark, red, blue and
  white

His mad dreams fought with waking life tonight

And of no such beauty, could he ever see again.

HAPPY EVER AFTER

1st SEPTEMBER

"Was it fate or was I just really lucky?"

Denzel's wife, Mary, asked those gathered for his eulogy.

"All I know is thirty four years of marriage to Denzel had enough love to fill the rest of my life ten times over. But I won't lie to you, when I met him as a freshman in high school, I thought he was the most annoying person on God's green earth."

Max laughed along with the teary-eyed crowd, clutching her aching rib. She had bruises like a peach from the explosion but was determined to make Denzel's funeral, and be a part of his three-volley salute.

"Honestly, he kept trying to impress me with how many points he got for the basketball team, or, somehow giving me advice about braiding women's hair, while I was just trying to learn algebra. But, when they're the one, they're the one."

Mary paused and gracefully observed the sunny heavens.

Max wondered how the woman could be so gracious when bitterness filled her own heart. Mary was just how Denzel described his queen and how Max imagined, ebony and beautiful, with style like an old Hollywood star. Behind oversized dark shades, she carried poise to the proceedings.

"Now there's a lot I could say about how Denzel passed, but I want to thank the Lord our son was late arriving home and that I was in the garden. Denzel will live on through all of us. He devoted his life to serving the community and died a hero. That's something worth cherishing today…

People would ask Denzel how he could be a policeman as a black man in America? With all the past racism and police brutality? But for him it was simple. Denzel wanted to be the change. So we will not seek an act of violent revenge for his death. We will rise above like Denzel."

At least one hundred people had made the outdoor funeral, with many more donating to public fundraising for the family, standing at over $20,000 so far. Alongside Max, Chief McCormack bowed her head. They tried to keep composed, after all, if Denzel's family could hold it together, they felt obliged to. The trouble was, they also felt guilty for his murder.

A pipe bomb was used for the explosion, homemade but intricately put together, without a trace. Determining a motive was also proving difficult for them. Over thirty years on the force involves a lot of grudges. Since Denzel's death, Max had recurring nightmares of dying in the explosion too, and woke still wondering what she could have done differently. All they could do today was fire three blank rounds into the sky, but like the battles of old, this sign meant the war could resume - at least for Max.

After the funeral procession, she and Chief took a slow walk along the church courtyard to catch up.

"I hear you're retiring?" Max broke the ice.

"Well that's got around pretty quickly," replied Chief, "yes, I think it's time. I made it to twenty seven years, a few shy of Denzel's total but I think it's time to check out."

"Congratulations Ma'am, we'll all miss you," said Max, beaming but devastated, "how will you enjoy your retirement?"

"Well," said Chief, taking a lily as they walked, "at first I think I'll just enjoy doing nothing, it feels like it's been a while since I had nothing on my plate. And, next week I'm very excited to be taking my niece to her first ever concert."

"Oh wow, amazing, Meat Loaf?"

"I wish, apparently Taylor Swift is whose cool these days."

Max almost keeled over laughing at the thought of Chief head-banging beside tween fans.

"Hey," Chief cracked a smile with her, "I've been doing some research and she's actually not that bad."

"Yeah it should be some show," Max giggled, "but seriously, no, it's actually so cool that you and your niece can share this experience."

"Oh wait until she hears me singing."

With laughter in the air, the tension lifted, though as they circled back round to the group, there was something Chief still needed to confess.

"And thank you Max, for being a great colleague, it's been a pleasure, really."

"Likewise, you have taught me so much."

"Well, I did my best… but do you want to know the real reason I'm retiring? I remember asking you and Denzel to trust me, to keep your heads down on the task and whatever happens rest assured, when it's all over your real lives are still waiting for you at home…"

"We all sign up for the risk Ma'am, it could never be your fault."

"All I know is I spent nearly thirty years putting off my real life. For all the people we helped, it was worth it. But I lost a marriage along the way and time with my children. And I didn't need to. You were right to worry about Alicia when shit hit the fan."

"There's no success without sacrifice. Do you know who also said that? A wise old lady called Niamh Cindy McCormack."

Relief washed over Chief. She always hoped she was making a positive impact on Max, but it was another feeling altogether to hear this from her.

"Okay more importantly who revealed my full name?" joked Chief, "No one has said those three words since my school teacher. And did you just call me old?"

They chatted like old friends instead of colleagues for the rest of the funeral, sharing their best Denzel stories with the crowd and crying bittersweet tears by the end of the day. And when it was time to say goodbye, hugged each other with a knowing embrace, for all the things still left unsaid.

Max made her way home to Downtown LA, struggling to process recent events. The funeral offered some closure, yet she was still waiting for the lesson from Denzel's death. She drove by familiar places and faces on her usual commute, questioning if she could really return to her daily life, in the full knowledge that the world would go on anyway.

Alicia kissed her hello at the door. A mess from her twelve hour nurse shift, but a sight for Max's sore eyes. She placed work into the back of her mind. Tragedy had reunited them. At first arbitrarily, but she now had genuine hope they could understand each other. Pain had made Max not care about hurting Alicia with the truth. About her childhood trauma, fears for the future and little bugbears. It was all Alicia needed to hear.

After a routine dinner, Alicia went to bed early, allowing Max to quietly slip out her work laptop in the kitchen. There had been a development in the Franco Egan case. Forensics had matched DNA from Franco's murder to the samples found on Donnie's strangled neck. To the police, however, Leon's identity remained a mystery.

First, they received a distressed call from a member of the public witnessing Ellie's kidnapping from the hospital parking lot, and were able to trace her phone location off pinging cell towers. A raid on an abandoned office off 61st Street produced a surprise body and Ellie's phone in his pocket. He was without identification and no one had reported him missing. For a day or two they were left with a John Doe, but when police began investigating Ellie's attendance to a psychiatric hospital, Dr Radford was able to identify the body as Donnie.

Abandoned at birth by a fifteen year old mother, son to a schizophrenic father already behind bars for sex crimes, Donnie was raised by his grandparents in Kansas. Until he set fire to their apartment on his fifteenth birthday, and ran away from home for good. The rest of his whereabouts were unknown until his death.

As for Ellie, the police had been able to determine by blood splatters and CCTV that she likely dragged the body of their bleeding mystery man out of the door and drove away in his 1969 Pontiac. They had doubts as to whether he could still be alive, judging by the amount of blood loss. They lost track of the car as they headed South. To the Mexican border? Thought Max. It was too early to say, she conceded.

She also wondered whether Denzel had been caught in this sprawling murder trail. After all, he was the SWAT leader during the raid when they found Franco's body. But she knew she was clutching at straws.

Max opened a recovered file from Ellie's cell phone and saw Leon.

"What's that noise?" called Alicia.

Max's shock had dropped a glass beer bottle on the ground.

"Nothing."

It's him, she screamed inside. The guy from the car chase. The wanted suspect in relation to the Los Muertos Cartel killings. She was hit by a serendipitous feeling of fate. Kind of hopeful, kind of haunting. If only they had caught him before.

She clicked through happy-couple pictures of Ellie and Leon. Selfies in sunglasses at the beach. Lunch dates for sushi at a fancy restaurant. Car ride karaoke videos at night.

She wondered, who was the hero or villain in this case?

Who was the hunter or the hunted?

She had accidentally stepped into their crazy world two feet first, but Max wasn't about to leave. She would find Leon and Ellie for answers. It was her turn to be the hero and hunter.

She went to bed and planned to wake up with a new purpose. No longer taking a back seat in her own life. Time to exorcise demons. She dreamt she died in the explosion with Denzel again, but it was the best sleep she ever had. The first sleep for the rest of her life.

ABOUT THE AUTHOR

Christopher Da Costa

Learn more about the Author and buy First Sleep: Volume Two via DaCostaBooks.com